MARK BANNERMAN

LEGACY OF LEAD

Complete and Unabridged

LINFORD
Leicester

First published in Great Britain in 2005 by
Robert Hale Limited
London

First Linford Edition
published 2006
by arrangement with
Robert Hale Limited
London

British Library CIP Data

Bannerman, Mark
    Legacy of lead.—Large print ed.—
    Linford western library
    1. Western stories
    2. Large type books
    I. Title
    823.9'14 [F]

    ISBN 1–84617–316–7

Published by
F. A. Thorpe (Publishing)
Anstey, Leicestershire

Set by Words & Graphics Ltd.
Anstey, Leicestershire
Printed and bound in Great Britain by
T. J. International Ltd., Padstow, Cornwall

For Bill —
in the hope that justice has been done

1

The squeal of brakes and the rattle of slowing wheels awoke Frank Miller, and he rose from the straw and moved across the cattle-soiled car. His head ached and his mouth tasted sour. He felt the train slowing beneath him as it took a tight curve. The sliding door was partly open, and he peered out and saw an immense expanse of sun-blanched prairie dotted with saguaro cactus. A hazy streak of purple mountains lined the horizon. Instinct told him that now was the time to quit the train, that, if he did not, sooner or later somebody would find him. For certain, the authorities would be alerted to his escape, beginning to ask questions in an attempt to piece together the route he had taken.

He turned back into the car, retrieved his convict's cap and placed it on his head. It wasn't the ideal headgear for a man running from the law, but with the noon sun burning down, he would need protection.

One thing he dreaded above all else was being sent back to the penitentiary. If he was, it would be for considerably longer than his original three-year sentence. Escaping from a work party, thanks to a sleeping guard and a wall that he had been able to scale, was not appreciated. And from the inside, he would never be able to prove his innocence.

The train was re-gathering speed as he made his jump, but he chose his spot carefully, finding a landing place where the grass cushioned his fall. For a long time he remained still. He was confident he had not been seen, not that anybody right here would be looking for him. But a man in a hoop-circled convict suit could quicken the interest of even a casual observer.

He listened as the rattle of wheels on tracks receded, and gradually the tangy smell of burning coal faded from the air, replaced by the pungent scent of sage. When he lifted his head, he saw the trailed plume of smoke against the azure sky and thought: *so far, so good.* He cautiously stood up and gazed around. *My God, scores of people rushing at me from every side!* He blinked hard and realized it was merely clumps of saguaro he saw, shimmering in the heat, with not a living soul amongst them. To the west, he noticed the glint of a stream as it caught the sun. He hadn't eaten for nearly forty-eight hours, and the only drink he'd taken had been from a cattle trough. He'd just concentrated on putting as much distance as possible between himself and the penitentiary. Now, his thirst was the most troublesome. He decided to head for the water.

He settled into a loping run, glad that he had regained his strength during the hours on the train. Coming across some empty freight cars of the Kansas-Pacific Railroad, still soiled and pungent with fresh manure from the cattle they had recently discharged, had been a lucky strike. It had been easy to climb aboard unseen, to bed down in the straw and be conveyed southward at speed. But now he had to rely on his legs again. Of course he knew that pretty soon he would need to exchange his prison garb for some less conspicuous clothing, and also get himself a horse, but with no money in his pockets, this wouldn't be easy. All he could do was wait and see what fortune threw at him.

Frank Miller was thirty years old and just under six feet tall. His head was close shaved, courtesy of the prison barber. His tough body was lithe, flat-bellied and wide-shouldered. His skin was a leathery tan, gained from many days spent beneath a hot sun, chipping granite with the prison chain-gang. The stubble lay thick upon his firm chin, and his eyes possessed the furtiveness of all hunted men. Sometimes during the torment he'd endured, he had wondered if he would

4

ever know laughter again.

The going was not easy through the grama grass with the sun burning his neck, rendering his clothing sodden with sweat, but he maintained a relentless pace until he reached the stream and plunged into it to drink and cool himself.

All his efforts had so far been aimed at getting away, but now he attempted to take stock and make some sense of the path he must follow. He calculated he was somewhere north of Abilene and west of Fort Worth, in Kansas. He would have to press on until he reached some settlement or ranch, where he could establish contact with human kind, and hope that news of his escape had not preceded him. He doubted that the law would bother to put a price on his head, because men sentenced for rustling cattle were small fry. That was in his favour, but he knew that the law did not like being made a fool of, and therefore he had no doubt that wanted notices with his name on would be distributed as a matter of routine. It would not be in his interest to attract the attention of any law-enforcement officers.

By the time the sun had settled into its westward drift and the sky had lost its starkness, Frank Miller had covered a further five miles and once, in the far distance, he had seen the brown of grazing Hereford cattle. He was travelling range land, which meant that sooner or later civilization, or those who frequented it, would put in an appearance. Meanwhile the only additional life he encountered came from cottontails, pronghorns, grasshoppers, a hovering buzzard — and once a diamond-back rattler that emitted a buzz, indicating that company was unwelcome.

Evening found him still without evidence of other humans, but that was to change.

As he topped a grassy knoll, he saw a valley with a stream running through, and on its bank stood a tumbledown shack. The sight took him aback, and he hunkered down and studied the place with wary eyes. To one side of the shack stood a crooked-looking privy. All appeared quiet, but a thin wisp of smoke rose from the shack's chimney. It must be coming from a cooking fire, for no sane man would require heat at this time of year. The thought of food had him salivating, licking his cracked lips. He figured somebody must be in residence, maybe a fence rider. Beyond the shack, he noticed a sorrel horse grazing. One thing was half-certain. This place offered two of the things he needed most in the world . . . food and a horse. And maybe more as well. He rose to his feet and approached with extreme caution, ready to drop to the ground at the first inkling of danger. As he drew close, he debated and figured the best thing would be to call out. What he didn't want was to surprise somebody so much they'd take a shot at him. So, raising his hands to his lips, he sent a friendly, 'Hello, there,' ahead of him.

He paused. There was no response, apart from the horse in the meadow lifting its head and nickering. Must be a mare. The opposite sex rarely nickered.

Frank swallowed hard, waited until the horse had resumed grazing, then he continued his approach. He had reached the open doorway, started to peer into the darkened interior, when a voice stabbed into his back.

'*Take one more step an' you're a dead'un!*'

2

Frank froze, cursing himself for not realizing that somebody could be spying out on him from the adjacent privy — somebody who obviously had a gun. What sort of fellow, he wondered, would go to the privy with a gun?

'Now what have we here?' The voice came again. It sounded asthmatic, wheezy, and extended into the splutter of a cough before continuing. 'An escaped jailbird, eh? Maybe there's a price on your head.'

Frank steadied himself. He still hadn't turned to see who was addressing him.

'No price on my head,' he responded. 'And I ain't got a single cent on me. Only thing I've got is this damned prison suit, and you're sure welcome to that.'

'Well, get your hands raised, mister,

and turn around real slow so's I can see whether you're worth shootin'.'

As Frank turned, his hands raised, he found himself gazing into the borehole of a rusty 45–70 Springfield. The man gripping it was suddenly overcome with a bout of coughing so severe that it seemed his guts might come up in addition to a spray of spittle. But despite the spasm shaking his corpulent body, his bloodshot eyes didn't flicker from Frank.

Frank was surprised by what he saw. The fellow sure didn't look healthy. He was wearing a filthy old shirt and his galluses hung down at his sides. His skin was a turkey-cock red, as if he was running high blood pressure. He was probably about the same age as Frank. He was egg-shaped with a great bulging belly and a disproportionately small head; and a straggly moustache spilled around his lips. His hair hung down in black strains, stuck to his face by sweat and an oily dewdrop had formed on the tip of his nose, growing bigger in readiness for its fall. Piss-stains showed on his old army pants. And now the stench of him drifted to Frank like a foul, invisible cloud. It would have broken a polecat's heart.

''You runnin' a fever?' Frank enquired.

The man dragged the back of his hand across his lips. His hands were strangely small, the fingers slim — like a pianist's or a gambler's.

'Just a damned cough,' he wheezed, 'but it ain't none o' your business. Now seein' as that you ain't got nothin' worth pinchin', and I sure ain't got no use for a convict's suit, I reckon I best put you out o' your misery.' He gestured aggressively with the gun. 'Like I said, maybe there's a dead or alive price on your head.'

'You won't get any reward for handin' me in, alive or dead,' Frank said, fencing for time. 'But I'll tell you what I have got. And that's an almighty hunger. I ain't eaten for a mighty long time. I would sure appreciate a little hospitality.'

The other man swore and scratched his jaw, his bloodshot eyes weighing Frank up. His grip on the Springfield had visibly slackened.

'Ok, Mister Convict,' he said. He turned his head slightly and spat out a wad of mucus, then he refocused his gaze on Frank. 'You're bound to say there ain't no price on your head. That don't make it true. Step inside and we'll talk some, and just remember I'll plug you if you get up to any fancy tricks.'

Frank nodded. 'No tricks. You got my word.'

His sick looking companion gestured for him to lead the way, and Frank stepped into the shadowy interior. The place was a tip, its earth floor covered in miscellaneous trash: old cans, bottles, mouldy newspaper, and what looked like animal excrement. But there were a few blankets in the far corner and the old stove was alight with a skillet of some sort of mush sizzling on the top. It made crackling noises and smelt of pork.

'You just passin' through?' Frank ventured.

'Sure, I am. You don't think I'd live in a stinkin' hole like this, do you?'

The gun had been lowered. For a time, a finger was still curled within the trigger-guard, but presently it was withdrawn and the weapon was leaned against the wall.

'You . . . best tell what you're about?' the big man demanded, his voice interrupted by more coughing. 'You can help yourself to some mush while you're at it. Not too much, mind you. I ain't no charitable society.'

Frank hooked a portion of mush from the pan, scorching his fingers but not caring. He blew on it, swopping it from hand to hand, then slipped it into his mouth. He'd never tasted better. The other man filled a blackened coffee pot from his canteen and set it on the stove, then he reached into a cloth bag and tossed Frank a hunk of bread, like he was dolling out a Christmas gift. It was stale, hard on the teeth, but edible.

13

'What name do you go by?' the man enquired.

'Frank Miller. What's yours?'

'It ain't none o' your business, Frank Miller, but I got nothin' to be ashamed of. My name's Cyrus Coppinger and I'm on my way to my uncle's ranch near Calico Crossing. You may have heard of John Coppinger's spread?'

Frank shook his head. 'I'm not familiar with these parts.'

'More used to the inside of a jail, eh?' his companion mocked him.

Frank said: 'I was put there for a crime I didn't commit.'

'They all say that,' Cyrus Coppinger commented, taking another portion of mush and waving it in the air to cool it. He stuffed it between his lips, wincing as it scorched his mouth.

'I never did what they accused me of,' Frank emphasised, 'and I intend to prove I'm innocent.'

Coppinger wasn't paying attention. He was too busy coughing and spluttering out bits of mush.

14

'You should take somethin' for that cough,' Frank commented.

'I do,' Coppinger responded. He reached down and unfastened a saddlebag that lay on a heap of blankets. From the saddlebag he produced a dark brown medicine bottle. 'Best brandy there is.' He uncorked it, gulped down a swig. 'Doctor told me it was the finest thing invented for chest sickness.'

He took another long swig, then wiped his lips on his sleeve. He re-corked the bottle and carefully placed it back in the saddlebag.

'Guess I still got room for a drop of coffee.'

He fumbled with the pot and makings, then drank Arbuckle's from a galvanized tin cup, after which he refilled it and passed it to Frank. It was scalding hot and black and thick as pitch.

Ten minutes later, Coppinger yawned and said, 'It's my restin' time. I got a busy day tomorrow, goin' to my uncle's ranch and all. He won't make me welcome, though.'

'Why's that?'

'He's dead as a doorpost, that's why.'

Frank said, 'Oh,' and watched as Coppinger lowered his cumbersome hulk onto the blankets. It seemed he no longer considered Frank a threat. Either that, or he felt too sick to worry. But he went through the motions.

'I'm keeping my gun right close to me, and I sleep awful light, and if you try any fancy tricks or try to steal anythin', then I'll shoot first and ask questions afterwards. We'll talk some more tomorrow. Understood?'

'Understood,' Frank nodded, resting himself down on the opposite side of the shack. He was as far away from Coppinger as the shack permitted because a sour odour emanated from the man and even at a distance was taking over from the mush-smell which had previously been prominent.

He wondered why this sickly man was so anxious to visit his deceased uncle.

Soon Coppinger was snoring, sometimes spluttering, like a grunting hog, but Frank was too bone-weary to allow it to disturb him. He felt himself drifting into sleep and made no effort to resist it.

★　★　★

Some hours later he came awake in pitch darkness, feeling stiff and uncomfortable. The ground was hard. He wondered what had awakened him and concluded that it was the intense quiet. He couldn't hear any sound coming from Coppinger's direction. No snoring, no coughing. Frank felt uneasy. Maybe his host wasn't there, had departed on some devious mission. Maybe he'd gone to fetch the law!

Frank climbed to his feet, as tense as a coiled spring. He eased across the floor, called the man's name: 'Coppinger!'

There was no response. But the unwholesome smell of the man hung in the room, somehow confirming that he was present. Frank reached the blankets, knelt down and his hand touched Coppinger's clothing, then his body. It was deathly cold and stiffening.

'Dead,' Frank whispered incredulously. 'Dead as mutton.'

He felt stunned; his immediate instinct was to get the hell away from this place before somebody showed up and started pointing a finger at him, accusing him of murdering this man. Could be he wouldn't get much time to explain that Coppinger had died of a heart attack or chest sickness or some other natural cause.

A thought occurred to him.

He needed a change of clothes mighty bad. Mind you, Coppinger's filthy garments would be about three sizes too big, and stank to high heaven, and were probably swarming with grey-back lice, but he didn't have much choice. Large clothing wouldn't draw so much attention as prison garb. So, with considerable disdain, he started to unbutton the clothing from the corpse, sensing that the body was growing stiffer by the second. Coppinger had soaked his pants with urine before expiring — or would it have been afterwards? When Frank had stripped the corpse, the paleness of dawn was showing through the shack's doorway.

The naked body looked like a pale mountain in the gloom and its sickly stink still polluted the air. Flies danced about it. Frank gathered up the clothing and stepped outside of the cabin. He glanced around at the prairie, shrouded in dawn's low mist, and could see nothing untoward. He noticed the sorrel horse standing motionless in the meadow and figured if there had been anybody else in the vicinity, the animal would have registered its fright. He went to the stream, took a drink and freshened his bristly face. He dunked the clothing, item by stinking item, in the cold water of the stream. He hoped that any lice and other assorted livestock would depart. When he had finished, he spread the clothing out on the ground so that the sun, when it came up, would get to work on the drying process.

On reflection, he figured it had been a stroke of luck, coming across Coppinger. The man had clothing, a horse, a gun and maybe some food supplies — all items he needed if he was to make good his escape and find the justice he sought.

He decided he'd best bury the corpse. If he didn't, the sight of it, lying in the shack, was bound to arouse interest if somebody eventually showed up. They might pick up his tracks. Anyway, he felt that he at least owed this man a burial. After all, Coppinger had voluntarily provided him with supper and a night's resting place, albeit somewhat curtailed.

He found a clump of wood and scraped away at the earth. Within an hour, he had a hole large enough to accommodate Cyrus Coppinger. He took a pride in it, as he did most things he undertook. Dragging the corpse from the cabin was backbreaking work and with the sun gaining intensity, he raised a considerable sweat. He stripped off his prison garb and laid it on top of Coppinger in the grave, then, naked, he scooped in the earth, stamping it down and making everything as inconspicuous as he could. He reckoned he should have said some prayer, but couldn't think of anything suitable for this man he'd known only briefly.

He wondered how far from civilization he was, where the nearest town or ranch was. Coppinger had mentioned a place called Calico Crossing, but right now Frank guessed he was on somebody's range, as he'd seen grazing cattle on the previous day. He decided he would continue westward and pray for good fortune.

He returned to the shack and found some bread and semi-rancid cheese. He wolfed it down, not harbouring fussiness about his diet. It was as he swallowed the last mouthful that his eyes fell on the saddlebags against the far wall — Coppinger's saddlebags. Conscious that they might contain something of value, he fumbled with the buckle, pulled back the flap and reached inside. He had hoped for more food or supplies, but all he pulled out were papers, the nigh empty rotgut bottle and a pack of playing cards. He dropped everything to the floor in frustration, was about to lift the saddle up and move out to catch the horse, when the official looking letter he'd cast aside caught his eye.

Elliot Freshman, Attorney at Law
Experienced in acting for the guilty
Calico Crossing

He stooped, gathered it up and his interest quickened as he scanned the written words.

Dear Mr Coppinger
I am holding the will of your uncle
John Coppinger who, as you may

know, expired recently. As you are his only living relative, he instructed me to trace you after his death and inform you that all his possessions, including his ranch and associated items, are to be passed on to you. I am aware that you are not a native of these parts, and have never met your Uncle John, but it is clear you were always in his heart. I must advise you that in order to claim your inheritance, you should visit my practice in Calico Crossing with this letter and adequate proof of your identity. The necessary legal process can then be set in motion.

Yours sincerely,
Elliot Freshman
Attorney at Law.

Frank Miller stood motionless, his mind suddenly racing with the possibilities, the temptations, that this letter presented. He felt the thoughts that drifted into his mind were sinful. But on the other hand, perhaps this was a chance that the Heavens had handed him, the gift that he'd prayed for? Or was the idea spinning in his head too fanciful?

The fact was that if Cyrus Coppinger had never before visited these parts, and was unknown, what was to stop Frank Miller, armed with this letter and any evidence of identity he could gather from the dead man's papers, going to that lawyer's office and posing as John Coppinger's nephew? But his conscience still pricked him. Despite being sentenced to jail, he had never committed a crime in his life. In years gone by, he'd been respected for his honesty, his integrity.

He slumped down, sitting by the grave, asking himself whether what he contemplated was a grievous sin — or a heaven-sent opportunity.

He consoled himself with the thought that there appeared to be no other living soul to inherit the Coppinger ranch, and nobody had a greater need than he did of a change in fortune and a new identity.

He pondered, and eventually reached his conclusion. He'd be a fool not to take advantage of something that had been presented to him on a plate.

He checked the saddlebags again, found a bundle wrapped in an oil-skin. This contained three hundred dollars in bills. There were also some more letters addressed to Cyrus Coppinger, then he found the man's birth certificate which he'd obviously been bringing to prove who he was. He grunted with satisfaction, went to pocket the documents but realized he was still naked. Coppinger's voluminous clothes were almost dry and he pulled them on.

It took him little time to gentle the mare and saddle it. The poor beast was run down, sharp-hipped and low of head, its ribcage standing out like the bars of a prison. Its left foreleg sported a white stockingfoot, otherwise its coat was dull sorrel. He returned to the shack, gathered up everything of value, including Coppinger's money, papers, rusty carbine, saddlebag and his battered, sun-faded fedora hat. Of course this was theft, but Frank salved his conscience with thoughts that Coppinger no longer had need for any earthly possessions.

3

He was riding westward, purely on a whim as he had no real idea of the lay of the land. All he knew was that he needed to find Calico Crossing if he was to put his outrageous plan into action. He was aware of his customary furtiveness, but realized that if he was to succeed he had to cast it aside and assume more bravado. He would achieve little by hiding now.

When he saw three riders coming over an adjacent ridge, his immediate impulse was to kick his horse into a gallop and take flight, but he reined in, telling himself that he was now a man called Cyrus Coppinger on his first visit to this territory and he was coming to claim his rightful inheritance.

He was sitting his horse with an enforced calm as the three came pounding up and halted in a swirl of dust. They were swarthy looking characters, all darkly moustached, obviously cowhands. If there was an ounce of spare flesh shared by the trio, the spare-hipped fit of the jeans and the loose hang of the hickory shirts failed to show it. They were all wearing belted guns. The foremost had an ugly scar across his cheek and he didn't mince his words.

'What you doin' on Amundson land, stranger. You ain't welcome here!'

Frank smiled and shrugged his shoulders. 'Well, I'm sorry if I'm trespassin'. I'm aimin' for Calico Crossing and I guess I got lost. I'd be greatly obliged if you'd point me in the right direction.'

His words seemed to take the three men aback. Hesitation cut through them. Frank decided to take the bull by the horns.

'My name's Cyrus Coppinger,' he said.

This revelation brought a strange reaction. The three all showed distinct surprise.

'Cyrus Coppinger!' The scarfaced man almost choked on the words.

'Sure,' Frank said. 'I guess you know my uncle's dead. I'm ridin' to town to tidy up his leavin's.'

One of the other men started to speak but Scarface waved him to silence.

'Well, you just ride over that far ridge,' he said, 'an' you'll see a river. Follow the river south an' that'll bring you to Calico Crossing. You can't miss it.'

'I'm real beholden,' Frank nodded, and heeled his animal away from the three in the direction indicated. For several moments he rode, feeling that their eyes were burning into his back. Shortly, however, he heard the pound of hoofs rising above that of his own beast and he risked a glance back. The three men were galloping off at a fair lick, as if anxious to impart some news they'd recently learned. Maybe, he thought, to their boss, apparently a man called Amundson. This prospect sent disquiet tingling through him. The three men had no more liked him than he had them, but for some reason they were playing him along. He shrugged aside his uneasiness, reached the river and continued his journey to Calico Crossing, passing through a number of out of town shacks where washing flapped in the drying wind. He noted how folks stood in their doorways, eyeing him, but he rode with his gaze fixed ahead. It had been some time since people had gazed at him and he didn't like it.

Ahead of him, the town took shape — a shambles of two storey white painted plank structures. He tensed as he spotted a 'wanted' poster nailed to a telegraph pole, but relaxed as he saw that the name on it bore no resemblance to his own. He passed a small cemetery with askew crosses. Ten minutes later he was riding up Main Street. It was nigh thirty yard wide and was lined with stores — *'Ibson's Cotton Shop'*, *'Pheobe's Sweets'*, *'Park*

Brewery', 'Indian Trading Post', 'Black-smith Shop', with an undertaker's parlour and so on. At the head of the street he reached the biggest building in town. *The Grand Palace Hotel*, and further along, beyond the Catholic church and *The Prairie Belle Saloon*, a much lower building with a shingle proclaiming '*Elliot Freshman, Attorney at Law*'. His pulse quickened. Within minutes his ruse might be blown sky-high. Alternatively, he might be on the way to the biggest slice of luck he'd ever known.

From within a saloon, the clink of glasses and loud voices sounded, but he ignored these, dismounted and hitched his horse to the rail outside of the lawyer's office. He took a deep breath and then stepped up onto the porch and through the open doorway into a shadowy office lined with heavy-looking books. A plump, bespectacled man was seated at an oak desk, busy scribbling on some papers. Frank had never seen a head so devoid of hair. It was like a naked dome. Frank rightly assumed that this was Elliot Freshman. The lawyer looked up, his shrewd, porcine eyes peering through his glasses, registering disdain. Frank felt uncomfortable at his dishevelled appearance and the fact that he was wearing clothing three times too big for him.

'Yes sir,' Elliot Freshman said. 'How can I oblige?'

Frank saw little point in delay. 'My name's Cyrus Coppinger. You sent me a letter regardin' my Uncle John's ranch.'

The lawyer's eyes narrowed to slits, but then reopened. For a second he seemed at a loss for words, but he regained his composure, stood up and stretched out his podgy hand which Frank shook

'Well, Mr Coppinger, you've certainly inherited a fine bit of land,' the lawyer said. 'Have you been out to look the place over?'

'Nope,' Frank said. 'I just rode into town. My first visit.'

'Oh yes?' the other man said,

somehow leaving the question hanging in the air. Then he went on. 'Of course while I in no way doubt that you are the genuine beneficiary of John Coppinger, I naturally have to have proof of identity before I can hand over the deeds.'

'Naturally,' Frank nodded, reaching into his pocket and bringing out the papers. 'Copy of your letter, my birth certificate and various other bits and pieces. I'm sure there's not much else you need.'

Freshman took the papers and spread them out on his desk, examining them carefully. 'Certainly seem in order,' he said, 'but I'd like to check them out overnight, and then tomorrow we'll get the marshal in and you can swear on the Bible that you're Cyrus Coppinger.'

'The marshal?' Frank enquired, trying to hide his agitation.

'Sure. He'll act as witness and that makes everything legal. Just a routine procedure. If you could come back here tomorrow morning, say about eleven,

I'll have the deeds ready for you and we can get everything sorted out. I'll hold on to these papers overnight. They'll be quite secure locked in my safe. Maybe you could get a room at the hotel.'

Frank forced himself to smile, though inside he felt downright queasy. 'Thank you, Mr Freshman. I'll see you tomorrow,' and he nodded and departed.

He walked the sorrel to the livery and settled it in, ordering a generous ration of oats, then he found a clothes store and fitted himself out with a shirt, levis, boots and 6-X Stetson. Freshly garbed, he went to the gunsmith's, pondered over a selection of used handguns and selected a Smith & Wesson Revolver, Model 1875. Its barrel was five inches long, and stamped on the right side of the heavy lug, under the barrel, was 'Wells Fargo & Co Express'. It came with belt, holster and ammunition. It would suit him fine.

Cyrus Coppinger's money wasn't going to last forever, but at least he had enough to keep him going for a few days. After that, he was hoping that Old John Coppinger would have included a healthy bank balance as part of his legacy. He just prayed that there wouldn't be any unexpected hitch in his plans. He somehow didn't trust the bald-headed lawyer Freshman and he would rather have got matters settled immediately rather than coming back tomorrow, particularly with the town marshal present, but he had agreed. The last thing he wanted was to raise anybody's eyebrows.

He bundled up Cyrus Coppinger's unwholesome garments and dumped them in a trash bin. Then he found a bath-house where he luxuriated in warm soapy water for an hour. After this, he stepped into the nearby tonsorial parlour and ordered a shave.

'Stranger in town?' the barber, a small, pale man, inquired as he stropped his razor.

'Sure,' Frank responded. 'First time I been to Calico Crossing.'

And then he took the bull by the

horns, figuring he'd got to show confidence in his new identity. 'I'm Cyrus Coppinger, John Coppinger's nephew. I've inherited his ranch.'

The barber unleashed a whistle of surprise, nicking Frank's chin with his cut-throat razor. 'Well, I'll be blowed. Everybody figured that as Old John Coppinger was short on relatives, the land would be up for grabs. Amundson has long fancied getting his hands on that land.'

'Amundson?' Frank queried. He recalled meeting those riders out on the range — Amundson's men, and they hadn't welcomed intruders. Was he going to have to resist encroachment from Amundson?

'Yup,' the barber nodded. 'He's the Norwegian who's got the biggest spread in these parts, but he's always wanted to get his hands on Coppinger's range. It's got the best water.' He swabbed the cut he'd made on Frank's face and stopped the bleeding. Then he said, 'It's been three months since Old John

Coppinger was murdered.'

'Murdered!' Frank was unable to suppress his surprise.

'Why sure. Didn't you know?'

'Oh yes. I knew all right.' Frank tried to cover up his surprise. 'A . . . an awful business.'

'The old man had the meanest temper I've ever known,' the barber said. 'Testy as a teased snake, with quick bursts of anger that scared the pants off you, but afterwards he'd be as nice as pie. No matter how mean he could be, he didn't deserve what happened to him. I sure hope they catch the bastard who did the killing.' The barber finished the shave, then handed Frank the towel.

Frank decided not to risk any further conversation in case he tied himself in knots. His hair was still prison-short, but now he felt less conspicuous and better able to face the challenges ahead.

He paid off the barber and found a café called '*Big Jake's*' where he ate a hearty meal of antelope ham and beans, followed by apple pie and coffee. He noticed plenty of glances coming in his direction, but he knew he would have to get used to this and not suspect that everybody was his enemy. A stranger riding in always aroused interest in a small community. He was still shocked at the news that Old John Coppinger had been murdered, but it was just as well he'd found out. He felt intensely impatient for tomorrow to arrive and another hurdle in his deception could be overcome. And then, armed with the keys to the ranch, he could ride out and begin life anew.

Or so he hoped.

4

Frank crossed the sun-baked street and entered the lobby of *The Grand Palace Hotel*, where he booked a room on the first floor and signed his name as Cyrus Coppinger. The shifty man who was hotel clerk seemed suddenly beset with the jitters, but he said, 'Pleased to have you here, Mr Coppinger, sir,' and passed him the key. Nodding his thanks, Frank returned to the street, figuring he would slake his thirst at the saloon to help the time along.

The Prairie Belle was fairly empty and smelt of rough cut and burley. He ordered a bottle of beer and the barkeep served him and said, 'Thank you, Mr Coppinger, sir.' Word of his presence was sweeping through town quicker than a brush fire on an August day. He sat at a table in the furthest corner, taking his time over the beer. As the evening developed, a crowd of cowboys came in and Frank got the impression they were from Amundson's spread, although none of them were the riders who had directed him to town. Soon he got tired of their foul-mouthed, drink-fuelled banter, and left the saloon without receiving attention. It was now getting quite dark.

He was walking back towards the hotel, when the shot cracked out.

Instinctively, he threw himself to the ground, not certain whether he'd been hit or not. Subconsciously, he'd been aware of the angry whine of lead and orange spurt of gunfire from the shadows across the street. Now he was sprawled face down in the open, utterly vulnerable to a second shot should it come. Caution had him laying still, convincing himself that the initial bullet had missed him, but sure that playing dead was his best form of defence.

Somebody had taken a shot at him, tried to kill him, but why?

And then, quite suddenly he was

conscious of approaching footsteps strangely mincing and short-paced. He struggled to keep motionless, quelling his breath. The footsteps stopped and he knew that somebody was standing over him — and he felt the awful pressure of a gun barrel against the back of his head. My God! He was about to be shot and now it would be impossible to miss.

He could hear the boom, boom of his racing heart, the pound of blood in his head. Surely his attacker must also hear.

An awful eternity seemed to pass; he was about to hurl himself over, struggle in a last ditch effort for his life, when the pressure of the gun was withdrawn and the footsteps moved away. He sucked in air, conscious that the ground beneath him was soaked with his sweat. Slowly his heart steadied and his racing senses subsided. He sensed he was no longer threatened. He'd been left for dead, which he would have been but for the grace of God.

He pushed himself up and scrambled to a point behind a post that offered some shelter. He stayed motionless for several minutes, his gun at the ready. The only sounds he could hear came from the down-street saloon — the tinkle of an off-key piano, a woman singing 'Tassels on my Boots!' and raucous laughter. If anybody had heard the shot, they weren't letting on. He watched the opposite side of the street until his eyes ached — but learned nothing of his assailant. He wondered if it was one of Amundson's men, one of those whom he'd encountered on the range. They'd certainly not been in the saloon with their bunkies. Maybe Amundson still hankered after the Coppinger land, and wanted him dead. Maybe Amundson had been behind the murder of Old John Coppinger. But whoever had taken the shot at Frank had vanished into the darkness.

Presently, after he had cautiously returned to the hotel and was in his room, he discovered the bullet had passed clean through the brim of his new hat, and he figured that he now had some sort of score to settle.

He was glad he was on the first floor, but if anybody was really anxious to have another go at killing him, they could shin up the outside porch posts and shoot at him through the window. With this in mind he quickly turned off the light, closed the window, and bundled some blankets in the bed to give the impression of a recumbent figure. He then leaned back in a chair in the corner of the room, his gun in his lap. He did not sleep. There seemed not a breath of air in the hot room, and anxiety increased his sweat. But he could have relaxed, for there were no untoward events during the night hours.

Bleary-eyed and tired, he was up at the crack of dawn, splashing water into the washstand bowl, cooling his face. His gaze lingered on the bullet hole in his hat brim and he shuddered. A couple of inches closer in, and all his troubles would have been a thing of the past.

Later, he heard the street coming to life outside, the clip of hoofs, the creak of wagons and men's voices. He sat the hours out, even foregoing his breakfast in *Jake's Café*, not wishing to risk his life unnecessarily. Eventually he heard the town clock strike eleven and he knew he had to face his next hurdle.

★   ★   ★

Checking that his Smith & Wesson was loaded and ready, Frank went down the hotel stairs and out into the street. He wondered if he should report last night's attempt on his life, but decided against it. It was about fifty yards to the lawyer's office and he remained vigilant as he moved along the sidewalk. The numerous women who were out, their shopping baskets on their arms, eyed the gaunt stranger, some even nodded a polite, 'Good mornin',' and he touched the brim of his hat. He decided that he needed friends and the best thing he could do was show courtesy to the locals. This had always been his natural manner, anyway.

He reached the open doorway of the lawyer's office, and steeling himself stepped inside. The bald Elliot Freshman rose from behind his desk with a beaming smile. 'Nice to see you, Mr Coppinger,' he said, and then for the first time, Frank noticed the grey-haired man standing in the corner of the office. He had squint lines around his eyes like spider's legs and a large cookie-duster moustache hid his lips. He was wearing a bright red bandanna, leather cuffs, and there was a lawman's badge pinned to his vest.

'This is Marshal Rainbird,' Freshman announced. 'He's come to witness you take the oath regarding your identity. That'll make it all legal.'

The marshal nodded a greeting and said, 'My pleasure, Mr Coppinger.'

Meanwhile Freshman had taken a Holy Bible from his drawer. He placed it on his desk and asked Frank to rest his left hand on it and raise his right.

Frank complied. He felt his insides trembling. He was about to commit sacrilege.

'Repeat after me,' the lawyer instructed. 'I swear before God that I am Cyrus Coppinger, the nephew of John Coppinger, and that I am entitled to his heritage as detailed in his last will and testament.'

Frank's uneasiness grew, but he took a deep breath and as he lied upon the Holy Book, he hoped that the Almighty would understand that he was locked into something he couldn't back out of. Maybe allowances were due, as previously he'd been treated with such injustice.

'Well, that chore's done,' Freshman said, slipping the Bible back into the drawer. 'Now there's just the identification document to be signed and witnessed and then matters can proceed,' and he coughed behind his hand in what Frank considered a strangely nervous manner.

Frank took the offered pen, read through the legal paper and duly signed the name 'Cyrus Coppinger'. Thereafter, Marshal Rainbird appended his name as witness.

Elliot Freshman moved around his desk, suddenly distancing himself from Frank, who immediately sensed he'd been lured into a trap. With smooth ease the marshal slipped his gun from its holster and levelled it at Frank.

'Get your hands raised, Coppinger,' he cried. '*I'm arrestin' you for the murder of your uncle!*'

5

Frank was speechless. The marshal was holding his gun as if he wanted to use it. The lawman stepped forward and, with his free hand, relieved Frank of his own weapon, tucking it in his belt, then he said, 'Hold your wrists out in front of you.'

'But, Marshal, I . . .'

'Do as I say,' Rainbird interrupted, 'or things'll be bad for you!'

Frank realized the futility of objecting. He positioned his hands as he'd been ordered. Within seconds he'd been cuffed.

'I'm sorry I had to turn over one of my clients to the law,' Freshman was simpering, 'but I guess it was my duty as a law-abiding citizen.'

'Quite right, Mr Freshman,' the marshal concurred.

'Of course his claim to the ranch will

be invalid, in view of his crime,' Freshman explained.

'Sure thing,' the marshal said, 'seein' that he'll most likely hang.' He turned to Frank, his face as mean as sin. 'You just took an oath and proved yourself guilty. Now start walkin', and do as you're told. I'll plug you if I have to, like you did your uncle!'

Frank knew that it was pointless arguing. He was obviously being arrested for a crime that the real Cyrus Coppinger had committed, and having just sworn on the Bible that he was that same person, all his plans had come tumbling down.

Feeling the prod of Rainbird's gun in his back, he walked through the doorway and out into the street where a number of folks and a dog looked on with puzzled eyes. Right now he wished he'd never set sight on the real Cyrus Coppinger, never hatched up the crazy scheme.

Five minutes later he was locked in the town's jail.

The whole sequence of events had stunned him. He'd feared that he might run into some sort of trouble, that somehow his ruse might be discovered, but he'd been hoisted on his own petard. His next action might well be attempting to persuade the authorities that he was *not* Cyrus Coppinger, rather than that he was. It had never occurred to him that Cyrus Coppinger might have murdered his own uncle. But how and why?

Marshal Rainbird was in no mood to listen to anything Frank might say. In fact, having consigned his prisoner behind bars, he absented himself from the jailhouse, leaving guard duties to his young deputy, Andy MacDonald. The latter sat at the desk, oiling his rifle, saying nothing. Frank too remained silent, beyond asking for a drink and being supplied with it in a wordless fashion.

The air in the cell was stifling, but he was no stranger to discomforts associated with being behind bars. Everything seemed to have happened so quickly, and now he slumped on the cell's wall-bunk and tried to reason out what had happened and what he could do to extract himself from this mess.

The real Cyrus Coppinger, before he died, had given Frank the impression that he had never before visited his uncle's ranch or the town of Calico Crossing, but clearly he must have been lying, though it seemed that nobody had seen him close enough to realise that Frank was an impostor. Cyrus Coppinger, however, must have slipped to the ranch to kill his uncle — if indeed the murder was a true fact. The whole business was utterly confusing, all coming on top of somebody trying to gun Frank down on the previous evening.

Why the hell had he chosen this territory in which to vacate the train — and why had Fate led him into a meeting with a man who was in the last hours of his life — and a criminal to boot? As if he hadn't had enough troubles already!

Finally, he gave up trying to fathom things out, and leaned back on the hard bunk. He hadn't slept at all last night, and now at first, he was reluctant to close his eyes because he was conscious that the cell's small window, strongly barred as it was, opened directly on to a side alleyway and any passer-by who fancied poking a gun through those same bars would discover that he was a sitting duck. None the less, weariness eventually overcame him and he slept.

He was presently awakened by Andy MacDonald, pushing a mug of stew through the bars, and he got his first good look at the deputy. MacDonald was scarcely out of his teens, though from his size you'd have figured him older, for he was a good six feet tall, thick-muscled and broad shouldered. His hair resembled a shock of rebellious hay, and he had an open, honest face. It was clearly pointless to attempt conversation with him, for he would divulge nothing without Marshal Rainbird's authority.

Frank rose stiffly from the bunk, taking solace in the fact that nobody had attempted to blow his brains out while he slumbered. He accepted the tin of stew with a nod of thanks.

He realized that it was dark outside.

As he ate, he wondered if Marshal Rainbird was arranging a trial, and stacking the odds against him at the same time.

Presently, MacDonald brought him some coffee and at last broke his silence. 'I hear you're gettin' a good defence lawyer, Mr Coppinger. Elliot Freshman's been appointed.'

Frank grunted with displeasure. He remembered the recommendation on the lawyer's letter. *Experienced in defending the guilty!* It hadn't mentioned what his success rate was.

It was an hour later that MacDonald called out, 'Wake yourself up! You got a visitor. Mr Amundson is here to see you.'

Frank rose from his bunk. The only light came from the gas lamp on the office desk, but as the keys rattled in the cell door, he became aware of the tall austere figure that entered, a man whose features were cloaked in shadow, but whose hair showed white in the gloom.

'Andy MacDonald,' the visitor called in a guttural voice that was clearly foreign, 'bring that lamp in. I need some light to see exactly what scum we have here.'

Frank recalled that the barber had told him that the rancher was Norwegian. *Why the hell is he paying a visit?*

'Yes, Mr Amundson,' the deputy responded, hurrying to comply.

The light arrived accompanied by a big moth, and gave Frank little comfort. He'd always felt there was something formidable, even sinister, about Amundson. Ever since he'd met those riders on the range. Now his suspicions were confirmed.

The Norwegian's heavy-browed, big

featured face was as gaunt as winter. He gazed at Frank for a long time, as if sizing him up.

'Well,' he said at last, 'you must know you are a certain thing for the hang rope. The whole town reckons you are just about the lowest scum on earth after what you did to Old John Coppinger.'

'I didn't do anythin' to him,' Frank argued. 'I've never seen him in my life. Why should I have wanted to kill him? I've never even been in this territory before. The situation is downright crazy.'

Amundson emitted a scornful laugh. He glanced over his shoulder, to make certain that MacDonald was out of earshot. He dropped his voice and said something that surprised Frank. 'I know you did not kill John Coppinger.'

Amundson paused for a while, then in even quieter voice he said, 'There's only one person in the whole world who can get you off.'

Frank's ears perked up. 'Who?'

Amundson stared full on into Frank's eyes.

'Me!' he said.

Frank's mouth fell open. 'How come?'

'Never mind about how come. You can leave that to me. But if I help you out, Mr Coppinger, I will require a favour.'

'A favour?'

Amundson didn't respond immediately. He rubbed his big jaw, still sizing Frank up, then he seemed to reach a conclusion.

'If I get you off this charge,' he finally announced, 'I want you to make me a promise.'

'How can you get me off?' Frank demanded, growing tired of the cat and mouse game Amundson was playing.

'I told you to leave that to me. Let me just say, I can produce a witness to Old John Coppinger's killing,' he said. 'Somebody who will swear that it was not you who did it. And in return, I will ask you to do just one thing.'

56

'And that is?'

'Take my daughter Elsa for your wife!'

Frank gasped, flabbergasted. He was lost for words. Why the hell should Amundson suggest such a crazy thing!

'We've . . . we've never met each other,' he at last managed.

'That does not matter,' Amundson said. 'She is a shy girl, not the prettiest but she will make a good Norwegian wife. And there is no desperate rush for a month or two. You court her and let things develop naturally. But she must never find out you and I have arranged things. If she did ever find out, then you will wish that I had let them hang you. I will give you six months to get the knot tied with Elsa.'

'But she may not like me,' Frank gasped.

Amundson drew a deep breath and then said: 'The truth is that as you come from the same stock as Old John Coppinger, you will be trustworthy like he was, good enough for her.' But his words sounded somehow clipped, as if getting them out hurt his mouth.

'From what I've heard,' Frank said, 'he wasn't exactly loved in these parts.'

'Deep down, he was a God fearing man,' Amundson said. 'And there's something you had best bear in mind. If you do not play your part, my men will show you no mercy. That's a promise I give you!'

'Why . . . why are you so desperate to get Elsa married off?' Frank asked. 'It makes no sense.'

'When you see her, you will realize that she is not every man's ideal woman — but we will cross that bridge in due course. You have got to make the choice. Oblige me with this small favour — or hang. Seems to me it is a simple choice.'

Frank looked at the Norwegian in bewilderment. True enough, it didn't seem he had much option but to play along with this crazy idea.

After a moment he said, 'All right, Mr Amundson. I guess you hold the whip hand. I'll do as you say.'

Amundson gave a satisfied nod. He reached out a leathery hand. 'Shake on it, Coppinger.'

They shook.

After Amundson had departed, Frank wondered what crazy events awaited him. What had he let himself in for?

There was one fact that lay in his mind like a prickly burr.

He was already married.

6

Over the next four days, Frank could do nothing but bide his time, suffer incarceration in that sweat-cage of a jail and attempt to ignore the frustration that plagued him. Marshal Rainbird only occasionally visited his office, leaving the day to day running to Andy MacDonald. When he did appear, he had neither word nor glance for his prisoner. As for Amundson, Frank couldn't guess at what the man was up to, but he was still reeling from the rancher's amazing proposition and instinct warned him that there was something downright devious afoot.

Then on the fifth day Marshal Rainbird arrived, a seemingly changed man, for his weathered face was creased with a smile. He immediately unlocked Frank's cell.

'Case is dropped,' he said. 'You're a

free man, Cyrus Coppinger.'

Frank chewed that over, suspicion seeping through his mind.

'How come?' he enquired.

'One of Amundson's cowboys saw Old John Coppinger gunned down. Swears blind it weren't you. Says he saw you in the saloon the other night. So you're a lucky man.'

Frank grunted with amazement. So Amundson was keeping his side of the bargain.

Now Frank had to come up with an impression that he was complying with Amundson's strange wishes. Alternatively, he could high-tail out of this territory at the earliest opportunity. He toyed with the option. His arrival in Calico Springs seemed to have stirred up a hornets' nest of intrigue that had almost cost him his life. But his fortunes appeared to have taken a lift. He was an inquisitive man, and the itch was in him to carry things forward, at least for the time being.

Accordingly, he took possession of

his bullet-holed Stetson, his gun, together with the cash and the other items that had been in his pockets when he'd been arrested. He felt he was walking on air as he left the jailhouse and, while his freedom sank in, he renewed his acquaintance with the barber. Afterwards, enlivened, he made his way to Lawyer Freshman's office, intent on completing his interrupted business.

Freshman was clearly aware of what had happened, for he waved Frank to a seat, even offering him a cigar which Frank rejected, being anxious to get down to the important matter of taking ownership of all that was lawfully due to Cyrus Coppinger.

'I'm really sorry about the misunderstanding we had,' Freshman smiled sheepishly.

'Don't worry about it,' Frank said. 'Let's just concentrate on gettin' the business done.'

The lawyer nodded.

By the time Frank stepped back into

the street, he had the large bunch of keys belonging to the ranch house, together with the authorisation to assume possession of Old John Coppinger's wealth which was lodged in the town's bank.

He spent a further hour setting up his new bank account, being welcomed with unstinting attention by the beaming bank manager. Thereafter, he had a hearty meal at *Big Jake's*, reclaiming the sorrel mare from the livery, and rode out of town, having been directed along the ten-mile trail towards the Coppinger Ranch. He could hardly believe that matters were running so smoothly.

★ ★ ★

The Coppinger ranch-house stood on a rise, dominating the trail. Frank rode through some tumbledown corrals, some scattered outbuildings that included barns, a bunkhouse and foaling sheds, and the silence hung about everywhere like a shroud. He reached the old white-boarded house, with tiled roof, bannistered verandahs and weed-choked steps up to the main entrance. The windows were boarded up. Once it must have been a fine residence, but now the whole place was on the way to dereliction, in desperate need of paint and carpentry work. It must have been allowed to deteriorate even before Old John Coppinger's death, and had slipped further into dereliction since, though in its day it must have been a thriving ranch.

Frank felt his old guilt. He had no right to this spread. It somehow seemed like opening up another man's grave. He sat on his poor looking sorrel, there in the ranch's yard, and let his doubts wash over him. Eventually he shrugged them off. This opportunity had fallen into his lap. He reminded himself, once again, that he would be a fool to disregard it.

Then he recalled his promise to Amundson regarding his daughter.

Could he risk becoming a bigamist? But he sensed that Amundson was a powerful man and once crossed he would be dangerous.

However, now he had to concentrate, quite literally, on putting his house in order and allowing the future to unfold in its own time. Also, he had not forgotten that his main purpose in escaping from jail had been to prove how unjust his sentence had been. Before he did that, there were a good many knots to untangle.

He dismounted, leaving his horse. Then, drawing the keys from his pocket, he climbed the steps to the porch, kicking aside the weeds. He unlocked the big door.

A minute later he had stepped into the subdued light of the main room. It was very grand, square-shaped, with a balcony leading around it on the upstairs floor. He could see that six doors showed where bedrooms led off. Everywhere was dusty, with the musty smell that indicated lack of human occupation for some time, but the potential of the place made Frank gasp. Within six months, barring unwelcome pressures, and a past that did not catch up with him, he could renovate this place, buy in cattle and labour, and turn it into a thriving establishment, perhaps to rival the neighbouring Amundson spread.

For a moment he was thrilled at the prospect, but then he took off his hat and saw the bullet hole in the brim — and he was reminded that he had an enemy who might even now be waiting to get another shot at him.

7

Over the next week Frank Miller took three trips to town and made purchases of paint and general supplies. He removed the boards from the windows of the house. Working steadily, he renovated and painted much of the property's flaking timbers and window frames, fixed the doors and then started to refurbish the outbuildings and corrals. He was a hard worker and took great pride in restoring everything. The house still possessed its furnishings, all well-worn but serviceable. In town he made enquiries regarding the purchase of a small herd of breeding cattle, a milk-cow and some poultry. He took on a veteran army corporal, Chet Evans, to help him with the chores. He also employed a plump Osage Indian woman, called Maria, for housework and cooking. She spoke no English, only her native Sioux language, but was remarkably cheerful, and always understood what he wanted. He knew that he would need more men when roundups and cattle drives were undertaken.

He rode out and explored his range. It was bigger than he had anticipated — maybe 50,000 acres. Rolling prairie, with scattered groves of trees and streams that spread across the land like veins on a man's hand, bordered on the eastern side by sprawling badlands. Within the thickets, he spotted a number of long-horn steers, wild as bobcats, and gave them a wide berth, not yet ready to tell them he was their new owner. Come next spring he planned to have them rounded up, herded to the railheads for sale in the north.

He reached a line of fencing, gazed beyond and guessed that what he was seeing belonged to Amundson.

He sighed, recalling the promise he had given the man and dreading the time when he appeared again. Or perhaps the Norwegian had played some crazy joke on him, for what reason he couldn't imagine. Particularly when Amundson hadn't first asked if he was already married. Demanding that a complete stranger marry your daughter was strange behaviour by any man's standards. Unless the daughter was some poor soul, long left on the shelf and so ugly that no man would look at her.

Frank shrugged his shoulders. Perhaps Amundson had already achieved his aims and would never show up again. Frank tried to convince himself, but somehow it wouldn't wash.

As the situation twisted and turned in his mind, his thoughts swung to his wife Lucinda — little more than a child when he married her, the apple of her mother's eye, dark-haired and pretty. Six years of marriage had not run smoothly, for she at times seemed irrational, sometimes naïve, and desperate for things he could not give her. He knew that he, too, had not been without fault. As it turned out, bizarre circumstances had forced them apart.

As the days went by, he struck up a friendship with an old timer called Fred Starret, who lived beyond the edge of the Amundson rangeland, and traded horses. Frank enjoyed doing business with him and found his stock fair-priced and good.

★ ★ ★

If Frank Miller cherished the hope that Amundson would simply stay on his ranch and that their paths would never cross again, he was awful wrong.

Frank took delivery of his cattle, chunky, red-and-white Herefordshire stock. With the aid of Chet Evans, he set about branding them with the same hog-eye brand that Old John Coppinger had used, and released them onto his ranges. The following week he had visitors at his ranch house.

Amundson, three of his cowboys, and his daughter.

They reined in their horses some twenty yards from the house. Frank had been seated on the veranda, enjoying his midday meal when he spotted them and a feeling of apprehension grew in him. This is what he had dreaded. It seemed that the past was catching up with him, albeit the recent past.

Amundson had been riding in a small buggy from which he now dismounted. Frank again realized how tall the man was, tall and somehow crow-like. But with a surprising chivalry, he turned and helped the young woman, who had been accompanying him, from her seat in the wagon. She was slim and willowy, wearing a calico dress of pale blue. Frank's pulse quickened as he guessed that this must be Elsa. He strained his eyes to catch a glimpse of her face, but she kept her head turned away, clutching the bonnet she wore as protection against the gusty wind — and she remained close to her father's heel, almost in his gaunt shadow.

But one thing was clear as a pikestaff to Frank Miller as the wind drew the girl's blue calico dress hard against her body, outlining the firmness of her breasts, of the nipples where they pressed against the cloth. Elsa Amundson was no old biddy!

Amundson's riders remained mounted, sidling their horses over to the water trough, but keeping watchful eyes on their boss and his daughter at the same time. Frank recognized the three brothers he'd originally met and wondered if one of them had tried to kill him on his first night in town.

As father and daughter stepped onto the porch, the girl at last turned her head, but Frank was no further enlightened, for she was wearing a veil.

'Welcome to Coppinger's Ranch,' he said, reaching out his hand to greet the visitors.

Amundson shook his hand in the familiar claw-like grip; a thin smile was on his lips. 'I'd like to introduce my daughter Elsa,' he said.

As Frank turned to the girl, she raised her veil from her face and what he saw gave him a distinct desire to gasp, but he suppressed it.

'When Elsa was a child,' Amundson explained, 'she was bitten by a dog. It disfigured her face.'

Frank nodded. He could not find the words of sympathy that perhaps he should have spoken, but the girl spoke up.

'Pleased to meet you, Mr Coppinger,' and her voice had the same Scandinavian accent as her father's. As she removed her bonnet, he noticed how her yellow hair was worn in braids that crossed at the top of her head.

'Like I said,' Frank said. 'You're most welcome here. Come inside and have a drink,' and then as they mounted the steps onto the veranda, he signalled to Maria to fix some drinks.

A moment later they were in the main room, cool and shadowy after the hot sun outside, and Maria fixed a jug of lemonade. As they sat at the table refreshing themselves, Frank allowed himself another glance at Elsa's face. No wonder she was shy and reclusive. A terrible scar extended from the edge of her eye, down across her cheek, slanting inward to disfigure her upper lip. It was ragged and shading purple.

The girl's eyes, which she had kept lowered till now, were suddenly raised to meet Frank's, and he realized that, disfigured as she might be, her eyes still retained a deep and purple beauty. Her hair was silky dark.

'Now, Cyrus,' Amundson was saying. 'how are you settling in? Fine land you got over this side of the river.'

'Things are goin' well,' Frank replied, but he couldn't shrug off his instinctive dislike of this man. 'Give me six more months and this place will be buzzin'. Just like it was in the old days, I guess.'

'You intend to stay here, then, and make a go of things?' Amundson wanted to know.

Frank wondered if this was somehow a loaded question. 'Sure,' he said. 'A man would be plum crazy to turn his back on a place like this. Maybe you'd like to have a look around, see the improvements we've made.'

Amundson gave another one of his tight-lipped smiles and nodded, and both he and the girl rose and followed Frank. He conducted them around the house and the outbuildings where he'd decorated and renovated things.

'You have worked hard,' Amundson said. 'You deserve all the good luck that has come your way.'

As they continued their tour, the girl lagged behind, finding interests of her own. Returning to the house, Amundson gave Frank a knowing nod, then turned to his daughter.

'Cyrus has requested a favour,' he told her. 'He says it gets very lonely for a man out here, and he asked if I would give permission for him to visit you, maybe next Sunday.'

The girl showed what appeared genuine surprise. For a moment she hesitated, then said, 'I would like that.'

75

Frank was taken aback, for he had indicated no such intention. However he knew that Amundson was enforcing his side of the bargain and it was clear he had to play along if he was to avoid trouble.

'Then we will take it as arranged,' Amundson announced, giving Frank an approving bob of his head.

Shortly afterwards, the visitors departed. As Frank watched the bunch of riders and wagon fade into the distance, he was left with an uneasy feeling. He couldn't puzzle out what Amundson was up to and he didn't trust him one iota. And as for his daughter? The poor girl had obviously suffered greatly with the terrible scar she bore, but there was something wanton about her young body — and her softly purple eyes had disturbed him. He wondered what would happen if Amundson was to discover that he was already married. He sighed. He knew he would have to keep the appointment on Sunday. If he didn't he had little doubt that

Amundson would put his threats into action.

For the remainder of the week, Frank busied himself on the ranch and undertook two trips to town to purchase supplies. But he was uneasy when he was away from the ranch, feeling that the townsfolk were watching him with questioning eyes, as if they suspected that he was not whom he claimed to be. And brooding over him was the recollection that somebody had tried to kill him. He knew that he was a sitting target each time he ventured upon the trail, or walked up Main Street, and in consequence his nerves remained on edge.

On the occasions that he visited the saloon, he gleaned some facts about the past and what he gleaned didn't make comfortable listening.

8

'Man to see you, boss!' Chet Evans called, poking his head through the doorway.

Frank was sitting in the big main-room, trying to make sense of his accounts. He glanced up and saw that a tall stranger had been ushered in by the ranch-hand. The stranger was power-fully built with arms thick as line-posts and hands big enough to match. The face was high of cheekbone, the oblique eyes as yellow as a sandpool bottom. But behind the hardness, was a friendly smile.

'Heard you were lookin' for men with ranchin' experience,' he said. 'Was wondering if I might fit the bill. The name's Dodson . . . Jim Dodson. Until recently, I ran my own spread down Sabine way, but locust ruined my stock, put me out of business, like a good many other folks.'

Frank stood up, eyed the stranger up and down and liked what he saw. He extended his hand. Dodson shook with a firm grip.

'Five dollars a day with food and accommodation,' Frank said. 'A month's trial to see if you make the grade.'

Dodson smiled. 'Guess that's the goin' rate.'

Frank nodded to Chet Evans. 'Show him around, then put him to work straight away. Guess there's plenty to get on with.'

'Sure, boss.'

Over the next few days, Frank was impressed with his new employee. Jim Dodson fitted in well with the rest of the crew, working hard. He also showed a good knowledge of the ranching business and at the end of his first week, Frank appointed him foreman of the ranch. He found himself drawn to the man, taking supper with him sometimes and liking the easy way he talked. He found his advice sound.

Twice he caught him roaring drunk and saw a more abrasive side of him, but chose not to hold it against him.

Then suddenly it was Sunday morning, and he remembered that he had an appointment to keep. He knew that if he didn't play along with Amundson's wishes, the man could make a lot of trouble — and trouble was the last thing he wanted. In consequence, midday found him giving himself a neat shave and putting on a smart suit of new clothes. He'd bought a pretty butterfly brooch for Elsa and hoped that she'd like it. He had to play the part of fervent courtier until he could think of an alternative plan.

He took his time as he forded the river, pausing for a thoughtful smoke before he set out on his ride across the Amundson range. The grass was alive with grasshoppers, pausing in their chatter as he approached, but resuming after he passed.

He had no idea of what to expect. The girl had said little during her visit to the Coppinger Ranch, but something in her eyes told him that she was no lightweight, that her face might be disfigured, but her brain was sharply focused. He wondered if she was somehow in league with her father, hatching up some evil plot that would prove his undoing. Or was she just a pawn in the game Amundson was playing? And what were his motives?

As he rode, he realized that the Amundson range was inferior to his own, at least in this section, for much of the land was dry and lacked the proximity to the river that he had.

By the time he reached the Amundson ranch house, he had encountered no signs of human life. He was sweating, partly from the day's heat, but more so from the apprehension that churned inside him. He exchanged nods with the several ranch hands he encountered. One man he recognized as having been among the original group he'd met when he'd first arrived. Back then they had directed him away from the Amundson range, indicating that he was not welcome. Now, the man's attitude appeared to have changed.

By the time he had hitched his mare at the water trough, Amundson himself was stepping onto the veranda to meet him, his tight-lipped smile working overtime.

'Glad you could make it, Cyrus,' he said. 'Elsa has been looking forward to seeing you,' and almost straight away the girl stepped out from behind her father. She was smiling, showing pretty, white teeth. She was wearing a split-skirt ready for riding, and a pretty blouse and a Stetson. A veil softened the scarred side of her face. The sight of her sent a glow of pleasure pulsing through Frank. Despite her ghastly injury, he found her strangely attractive.

He doffed his hat, and said, 'Real nice to see you, Miss Elsa. I have a few picnic items in my saddlebag, and was hoping we could take a ride, if the heat won't be too much for you.'

'The heat's just fine,' Amundson responded, speaking for his daughter as if he didn't trust her to respond in the right fashion.

At that moment, one of Amundson's men arrived, leading a handsome mare, saddled and ready to ride.

Nodding in Frank's direction, Elsa stepped from the veranda and mounted the mare with an easy grace, riding astride. She was obviously no stranger to horse-riding. And no stranger to looking after herself, Frank figured, despite her apparent shyness.

As they rode out onto the range, a change seemed to come over her, for she found her tongue in no uncertain manner. There was something about her Scandinavian accent that he found alluring.

'You must find it strange living out here, after what you have been used to.'

Too true! he thought and glanced at her anxiously — then he relaxed. How could she possibly know how close she was to the truth; that all his previous residence had offered was the cruel confinement of prison bars and the brutality of guards.

'Yes, Elsa,' he said. 'The climate is not so harsh here.'

'Where was your previous home?' she enquired.

'Wyoming,' he said, hoping she would not press him to be more specific. Thankfully, she did not, so he took over the questioning. 'How about you? You haven't always been here.'

'No,' she responded. 'I've been three years back east — at college. I enjoyed studying the great books and some-times we were taken to the theatre.'

'Then you must find it difficult, comin' back here.'

She moistened her lips with the pink tip of her tongue. He felt an urge to kiss her but restrained the impulse. 'No,' she said. 'I love this country, although sometimes I find it lonely.'

They talked on, gradually breaking down, Frank felt, the barriers to their acquaintance. He began to enjoy her company, for beneath her initial reserve he found a sense of humour and a pleasant manner. She was anxious to learn about him, but did not embarrass him by being pushy.

He said, 'Did you know my uncle?'

Her expression darkened. 'Yes. It was terrible, what happened to him. He didn't deserve that.'

'He sure didn't,' Frank agreed, but he had no wish to push the matter further in fear of venturing into areas of his ignorance.

They rode for an hour, finding that the time sped by. He gave her the brooch and her eyes lit up. She told him that the family had moved from Oslo when she was a child, that her mother had died as she attempted to bear a second child which also perished.

After they stopped for their picnic, some inner sense of Frank's warned him that they were being watched. He had noticed a quick flash of light coming from an adjacent ridge and experience told him that the sun had caused a glint on gun-metal.

'Are we being watched, Elsa?' he asked.

She sighed. 'I expect so. Father worries. He figures we need a chaperone, I guess.'

Frank grunted uneasily. He didn't like being spied upon. Especially by a man with a gun. Especially as he wasn't certain who his enemies were.

But whoever their chaperone was, he didn't trouble them during their ride back to Amundson's ranch. Frank didn't see Amundson again, but Elsa was insistent that he come over again on the following Sunday, and her purple eyes were sparkling and her face seemed happy, despite the fact that she retained the veil over the unsightly part of it. He reached out, gave her hand a squeeze and she held on for longer than he'd expected.

As he rode home, he cautioned himself. Elsa seemed a sweet and warm girl, so different from her father. Despite the predicament Frank was in he had no desire to hurt her. If she learned that he was already married, he guessed she would be deeply grieved.

Next Sunday, he again went riding with her and inwardly his heart melted towards her, but he didn't make any advances towards her. It wasn't because all along he suspected that there might be a man with a gun watching his every movement from beyond the adjacent ridge. It was because he was a married man, and despite the fact that he had fallen on difficult times, he had never been unfaithful to his wife.

The following month he told Elsa that he had to go East on cattle business, but he would get back just as soon as he could. Dismay flushed her eyes, tears glistened, but he knew he had no alternative. He had escaped from prison in order to seek justice. Of course he'd mentioned nothing of this to Elsa, nothing of the fact that he was living a complete lie. But his aim had not altered — and he had to sort something out with his wife, Lucinda. Somehow he had to mould the future so that it would sit easily with everything that had happened to him. But it was going to be difficult.

9

For days he agonized over what he should do. Should he confess to Elsa the whole truth, he wondered? He discarded the idea. He could not deny that he was becoming increasingly fond of her, yet he decided he could not reveal it to her. There was only one thing for it. He would have to return to Wyoming and attempt to sort things out with Lucinda, endeavour to establish the true facts behind his jail sentence and establish where his priorities lay. Returning to his home town of Clayton, Wyoming, would be dangerous, for he was still a wanted man, and the law had a habit of never forgetting, particularly now that telegraph lines were spreading across the land. Admittedly he could stay here, living in his fool's paradise, albeit a dangerous one, but he had the haunting feeling that things would not run smoothly for ever. Sooner or later the past would rear its ugly head, enemies would appear, and he would be obliged to fight to maintain everything he achieved over the past months.

Frank had grown increasingly reliant on Jim Dodson. His foreman appeared a good and reliable friend, having no more drinking bouts. So Frank took him into his confidence, feeling that he could trust him. He told him about how he had agreed to marry Elsa — even though he was already married, and that was what he had to go East to sort out. Dodson showed surprise at the revelation, but assured Frank that he would keep tight-lipped on the subject. Three days later he handed over the running of the ranch to Jim Dodson, packed his warbag and caught the stage to Milton City and from there boarded the train to the north. As he settled back into his seat, he recalled the last time he had travelled by rail — buried in straw aboard a wagon that still stank of the cattle it had conveyed. Certainly circumstances had changed, but leaving his ranch was still fraught with danger. He had altered his appearance as much as possible, allowing his hair to grow shoulder-length, and his beard, moustache and sideburns were neatly trimmed, but none the less covering most of his face.

The following day, he got off the train at Chinook City where he purchased a horse — a sturdy dapple-grey mare with a hogged mane. He rode the next fifty miles to Clayton, avoiding other folks as much as possible, for the last thing he wanted was to have to explain his presence. He camped rough overnight and next day, he reached Clayton and went straight to the home of Kezy Brooks, an old friend from his days as a ranch foreman at Clancy's.

Kezy was a fifty-year old bachelor, crippled with rheumatism and handicapped by the lack of his left eye, which he'd lost at Gettysburg. Sometimes blood-tinted fluid leaked from the socket, staining his cheek. He ran a hardware and saddlery business. He also fashioned horsehair hat-bands, watch chains, head stalls and bridles. He welcomed Frank with surprise and delight. Soon they were enjoying a meal together.

'You best be careful, Frank,' Kezy warned. 'Ever since we got news of your escape from jail, Marshal Dixon has been watchin' for you. But as far as I'm concerned, you told me you weren't guilty of thievin' those cattle, and that's good enough for me.'

'I'm grateful for your trust, Kezy.' Inwardly Frank felt a tinge of shame. Kezy Brooks would have been surprised had he known what had happened regarding the inherited ranch. Sometimes he concluded that he had ventured into dishonesty too easily — and one day he would have to come clean and somehow make amends. But he couldn't do it yet.

Kezy imagined that Frank had been

living rough since his escape, and Frank did not enlighten him. Instead, he enjoyed his friend's company. It was as they were finishing their meal with a bottle of wine, in a room decorated with leather-work, that Kezy grew hesitant. He kneaded his knuckles, wincing as he rubbed the misshapen bones. Finally he said, 'There's somethin' you better know, Frank.'

The tone of his voice sobered Frank.

'It's something you won't appreciate,' Kezy went on. 'Lucinda . . . well, she's livin' with another man.'

The words stung Frank. Things had been difficult between him and Lucinda, always had been, but he'd respected his marriage vows and he'd always felt certain she'd been the same.

'Who?' he gasped.

Kezy wiped his moustache with his polka-dot handkerchief. 'Three months after you went to jail,' he said, 'she moved in with Ty Beddows, over at his farm. Apparently, he'd been pesterin' her to do that for a long time.'

'She . . . ' Frank choked on his words, stunned. Then, slowly, he felt a deep hurt rise in him. 'I know she went over to Beddows a lot, but she said it was to see his sister.'

'Well, maybe that wasn't what she was doin', Frank. I guess when you were accused of stealin' them cattle and got sent to jail, Beddows had his way with her, persuaded her to move in with him.'

Frank buried his face in his hands, still trying to disbelieve what his ears were telling him. All the time he'd been locked away, he had thought that one day he would return to Lucinda, that she would help him to clear his name.

But now another idea was forming in his mind, and with it a simmering anger.

He got up from the table, reached out to shake Kezy's hand. 'I'm beholden to you,' he said. 'I'm glad you told me.'

'Don't do anythin' crazy,' Kezy advised. 'It ain't pleasant to pass on bad news, Frank, but I guess that's what friends are for.'

Twenty minutes later, Frank was on his way, heading his dapple-grey mare towards Beddows' farm. The fury burned inside him. He couldn't believe that Lucinda would have done this to him. Admittedly, life hadn't been easy between them, but he'd imagined that she'd been trying to overcome their problems as hard as he was. It was just that her ways were different from his, that she saw the world in a different way. While he had been behind bars, he had started writing to her, but she'd never been gifted with writing and gradually their correspondence had dried up. Now his anger was blended with jealousy. No man likes his woman stolen by another man.

He reached Beddows' farm in the early afternoon. The place was in a small valley a few miles west of Clayton. It was a clutter of old farmhouse, hog and chicken pens, a field of grain and a meadow in which some cows and goats grazed. He noted that the cattle he was supposed to have stolen had been replaced.

He could feel emotions hammering inside him, and he tried to calm himself. He knew that Beddows had the reputation for being a violent man, and he'd shot and killed a man a year back — in self defence, so the law had decided. Frank carried a gun himself, but he had never prided himself with the sort of skill some men boasted.

He left the mare rein-tied in a clump of aspens and approached the house on foot. He realized that he was blundering head first into a situation that could turn bad, but his anger made him determined to resolve the matter, by what means, as yet, he didn't know.

As he got near the farmhouse, everything was graveyard quiet, apart from the creaking that came from the sails of a small windmill. The house was a single-storey cabin that had been converted from the original soddy. At the back were a couple of sheds. He noticed that the cabin door stood open. Inside looked deserted and shadowed. He tried to calm his hammering senses.

From the yard, he called, 'Hello, there!'

For a moment there was no response, but he could hear the steady tick of the big grandfather clock that stood just inside the door. He started nervously as it chimed two o'clock.

He heard the movement of approaching footsteps, coming from the back of the cabin and he brushed the butt of his pistol with his hand, ensuring that the weapon was handy if he needed it.

But it wasn't Beddows who appeared before him. It was his own wife, Lucinda.

She looked gaunt, deathly pale, a shadow of the spirited, pampered girl she'd once been. As her large eyes settled on him, her face was filled with disbelief. Tear-funnels seared her cheeks. She tried to speak but all she managed was a parched croak. Her eyes took on a hazy look and she sagged forward as if fainting.

He had no choice but to catch her in his arms, to hold her, to feel the shudder in her body as she gasped for air. And for a second, holding her close, he remembered other times and emotion choked up in him.

'Lucinda,' he murmured, soothing her back, 'what's happened to you?'

'Frank . . . Frank!' she gasped. 'God has heard my prayers.'

She was clinging to him as if she would never leave go, her tears moistening the side of his face.

'How I've prayed you'd come back,' she sobbed.

For a minute, he let her ramble on, making no attempt to disentangle himself. 'Lucinda,' he at last murmured, 'how come you're here, when all the time I figured you'd be waiting for me at home? And where's Beddows?'

'He's gone to town on business,' she said, drying her cheeks with a trembling hand. 'It's so good when he's away. I thought he was a wonderful man, that he would look after me. I thought he was a gentle giant, but, my God, I was wrong. He's . . . ' She drew back, taking a deep breath, shaking her head in distress. 'I was such a fool. We had it good, Frank, you and I — but I was too stupid to appreciate it.'

'Lucinda, what you've done is terrible . . . '

'I know I've sinned,' she confessed. 'I'm asking for your forgiveness, Frank. I promise I'll be a good wife if you'll take me back.'

He swallowed hard. He didn't know what to say, but he could feel the anger draining from him.

After a moment he gasped, 'Lucinda, I escaped from prison. I'm on the run, hiding down in Kansas. I can't come back here. They'll arrest me, put me back behind bars. I'll always be hiding from the law, I guess.'

'No you won't,' she said firmly. 'I know you never stole those cows. I know everything was fixed to make you seem guilty.'

It took a second for the implication of her words to sink into his brain.

'Who fixed it?' he asked.

She took another breath as if steeling herself for what she had to say.

'Who fixed it?' he repeated.

'Ty Beddows did. He told me when he was in his boastful mood, just a week ago. He taunted me. You see, he figured with you in prison, he could have me all to himself. I know it was truly sinful. I should never have . . .'

'Oh God!' It was Frank's turn to gasp. 'And you didn't know he'd fixed things to make me look guilty?'

'Not until last week. I didn't know what I should do.' She glanced around the yard nervously. 'He said he'd kill me if I told anybody.'

She stepped away from him, slumped against the wall, sobbing with distress. He'd never seen her this way, never dreamed he ever would, and it cut him to the quick.

For a moment Frank stood non-plussed, then gradually the old compassion he'd always held for her seeped into him. He knew he'd always been soft with her, yet it had not been in his nature to be otherwise.

'Lucinda,' he murmured huskily, 'I need to think about things. I need time. I'll come back tomorrow. I feel real sorry for you, but . . .'

'But he'll be here tomorrow, Frank. Ty will go crazy if he sees you.'

Frank swallowed hard. He knew that Ty Beddows was a bear of a man. What Lucinda had ever seen in him, he couldn't guess.

But Frank had spoken the truth when he had said he needed time. Could he find it in his heart to forgive her for what she'd done to him?

Now he looked into her pleading eyes, deep, tear-shiny pools pleading with him. He noticed again the bruising on the side of her face. No doubt other parts of her body had also been abused.

'Lucinda,' he said, 'if I've got to face

him, so be it. I'll come back this time tomorrow. I'll let you know if there's any future for us. This has been an almighty shock.'

He wrenched his gaze from hers and turned. As he strode away from the house, he could hear her weeping, but he did not look back. Then, suddenly, her weeping changed to alarm. It came as a shrieked, '*Oh God!*'

Off to his left, Frank heard the sound of hoofs and glancing across he groaned. Ty Beddows was reining in his big bay horse just yards away, his heavy-jowled face red with anger.

'Well, if it ain't my old friend, Frank Miller,' he snarled. 'I don't welcome escaped convicts around here,' and almost imperceptibly he drew his ivory-handled six-gun, pointing it at Frank. 'The law will sure thank me for takin' you in — unless I have to kill you first.'

Frank debated whether or not he should make a grab for his own gun, but he dismissed the idea. Beddows would be faster.

Keeping the revolver unwaveringly aimed, Beddows slid from his saddle, his eyes glaring into Frank's. It was clear he wanted Frank to attempt to escape or to react in a way that would give him the excuse to open fire. But Frank froze where he stood, and behind him he heard Lucinda's pleading words. 'No, Ty. You know he's an innocent man!'

Beddows drew his lips back to reveal his teeth. 'He's scum,' he snarled. 'I told you that, Lucinda.'

'That's not true,' she said, showing defiance for the first time.

Beddows was breathing in great gulps, emotion making a pulse throb on his brow.

Frank knew that he was a simple trigger-pull away from death.

'I'm gonna take you into Clayton, Frank Miller,' Beddows said. 'Hand you over to the marshal so you can be put back behind bars where you belong. If you ever show up around here again,

I'll blow your damned head off. Lucinda's my woman now. You're a thing of the past. Get your hands above your head.'

Frank knew he had no option but to comply. He lifted his arms, and Beddows stepped forward and relieved him of his gun.

Next, he took a throw-rope from his saddle and Frank submitted as he was ordered to lower his hands, and his arms were lashed tightly to his sides. When Frank glanced back at the house, he could see that Lucinda had slumped to the ground, her body shuddering as she sobbed. It was clear she was terrified of Beddows, physically weakened by her ordeal, and was helpless to intervene on Frank's behalf, even if she'd wanted to.

Beddows remounted the bay horse, gripping the rope, forcing Frank to walk ahead of him like a dog on a leash. As he went forward, Frank risked one last glance in Lucinda's direction, and called out, 'My horse is tethered up in the alders. Set him free, Lucinda.'

Whether or not she understood, he had no way of telling. All he heard was Beddows' impatient snarl. 'Cut the cackle, Miller. You won't have need for that horse no more!'

It would be a long walk to town across rugged ground, cloaked with silver-grey sage-bush. Beddows started at an impatient pace, keeping his gun drawn throughout, snarling at Frank for greater speed. Frank acted in a submissive way, but his brain was working overtime. He had no intention of being handed over to the marshal, and no intention of going back to jail for a crime he hadn't committed.

10

Frank maintained the fast pace for as long as he could, knowing that Beddows would have little hesitation in shooting him if the slightest excuse presented itself. The going was demanding, particularly with his arms bound to his sides by the circled rope, which was so tight around his chest that it stopped the full expansion of his lungs. Eventually he stumbled. He desperately needed to take a breather. He heard Beddows' mocking laughter. The rope was jerked viciously, forcing him to stumble on.

After about an hour, they descended into a rocky ravine through which a stream meandered, and, as he called a halt, Beddows dragged Frank off his feet, grazing his knees on the sharp rocks. Beddows allowed his bay horse to drink, but as Frank attempted to do likewise, he again yanked on the rope and yelled out, 'No you don't, Miller. You don't deserve no luxuries!'

Fury boiled in Frank. The blood pounded in his temples. He glared at Beddows, seeing how he had hitched the end of the rope around his saddle pommel, slipped his gun into its holster and was fumbling with the makings of a rice-paper smoke. Frank sensed that it was now he had to make his bid for escape.

He drew all his strength together, unleashed a fearsome yell. He hurled himself away from Beddows in a desperate leap, exerting all his weight. The rope was taut between him and the saddle horn. The result was that the saddle was dragged from the centre of the animal's back. It nigh wrenched the breath from Frank's lungs, but he achieved his aim. The horse was panicked by the noise and sudden movement, whinnying wildly as it reared, unseating the surprised Beddows. He clawed for his gun, but never got the weapon clear of its holster. He plunged backwards from the displaced saddle and hit the rocky ground with a thud. Frank was dragged by the rearing animal, aware of excruciating pain in his arms, but somehow he got to his feet, and, finding himself standing over the prostrate Beddows, he dropped knees-first onto his enemy's head, aware of a cracking sound as he did so.

In the next instant he fought a desperate battle with the panicking horse, losing his own footing, being pulled over the ground. But shortly the animal steadied itself, slowed by the weight of the man it was dragging and finally stood still, its breath heaving as it became calm.

Dazed, Frank raised his head, saw the sprawled body of Beddows, saw the blood flowing from his skull. It looked as if his brains were oozing out. There was no movement in him, not the slightest rise and fall of his chest. Realization swept over Frank. He had never meant to kill the man, but he'd had little option.

He cursed the ropes that secured his arms. Using his legs as leverage, he clambered onto his feet, stepped close to the horse and murmured gentle, calming words. The horse snorted its disdain at the recent violence, but remained still, awaiting the next command. Frank noticed the quirt marks on the beast's flanks, and suspected that Beddows had been equally hard on Lucinda.

Awkwardly, working with hands, despite the fact that his arms remained roped to his sides, he somehow straightened the saddle on the horse's back. He glanced again at the body of Beddows and saw that his own Smith & Wesson had fallen from Beddows' belt. Leading the horse, he eased himself across and recovered the weapon. It was difficult working with his arms secured. Then he noticed the match box that Beddows had taken from his pocket to light his cigarette. Its contents were spilled out on the ground. An idea came to him.

It took him half an hour of frustrating work, and a score of matches, to achieve his intention. He scorched his hands countless times, but eventually he had started a small fire of twigs. It was painstaking toil, and at times he almost gave up, but finally he was able to burn the rope binding his arms, weakening the strands. At last he was able to break them apart and unwind the rope that encircled his arms and body.

He leaned back, breathing a sigh of relief, exercising the feeling back into his arms. But then he remembered Lucinda.

He mounted the horse and heeled it into motion. He had to get back to Beddows' farm. He had been wrong to ever think of leaving Lucinda — but thankfully she no longer had to contend with Beddows. At least that was the way he reasoned.

★ ★ ★

Frank's emotions were in turmoil as he drove his newly acquired bay-mount at a hammering stride back to the Beddows Farm, the tree fronds scraping against him. He knew that he still had a responsibility towards Lucinda, no matter what she'd done. He had a lot to forgive her for, but he told himself that what she had suffered through her infidelity had been a terrible retribution, and it was not in him to punish her further. For the moment he pushed events to the south. Elsa Amundson and her father, to the back of his mind. He could only cross one bridge at a time.

He reached the ridge overlooking the farm as dusk was descending. The farmhouse was unnaturally quiet. A sense of pending disaster settled on him, and he didn't know why. In the yard, he slid from the saddle and left the horse. The main door to the house stood open and he rushed through calling, 'Lucinda! Lucinda! You're safe now!'

He stood in the cabin, steadying his heaving breath. He was about to call again, but somehow the futility of it struck him. The place had the echo of emptiness about it. Lucinda wasn't here. This was confirmed by his quick rush through the several untidy rooms.

He had no wish to linger. There would be too many reminders of Beddows, too many reminders of the distasteful way Lucinda had been maltreated. What a fool she had been to be influenced by such a bully of a man!

Frank had no idea where his wife had gone, but as he remounted the horse the thought lingered with him that he had killed Beddows and therefore he would be considered a murderer. That he was escaping, once again, from lawful arrest, would make matters even worse. He debated what he should do, where he should go. If he returned to town, it seemed certain that the marshal would arrest him, send him back to jail. Only one person could testify that he'd been innocent of stealing Beddows' cattle; that was Lucinda — and she had disappeared, gone God knows where.

It was possible that Lucinda had fled in panic — terrified of Beddows and what he might do to her when he returned from delivering Frank into custody. She might be miles away by this time, unaware of Beddows' fate. Maybe she had gone home to her widowed mother in Custer City, fifty miles off.

Frank nudged the bay horse forward, momentarily uncertain which way to head and allowing the animal to take its own route. Of course he could board the train and return to the ranch in Kansas, return to Elsa. But meeting Lucinda again had reminded him that he still had responsibilities towards her. No matter how disgracefully she'd behaved, she was still legally his wife. And the thought that she might be somewhere in dire straits made him think that before he left this territory he had to settle things with her — one way or another.

He rode deep into the woods, the darkness thick about him, and when he was some miles from the farm, he unsaddled the animal, hobbled its forelegs and settled down for the night, using his gear as a pillow, covering himself with the horse blanket, thankful that the night was warm. He needed time to think. Presently, he gazed up through the tree fronds and saw the sky become stencilled with stars.

He didn't sleep much that night. His mind was too busy weighing up various options. One thing became clear. He must find his wife, and the only logical place to start his search must be where he'd last seen her. At the farmhouse. She might even have returned there of her own accord, though he doubted it. However, he might find some clue.

As the new day eventually came, bursting like a black sack to send the gold of dawn streaking across the distant mountains, he rose from his blanket, stiff and cold. He was hungry, but he had no food. Perhaps he would find some at the farmhouse. He consoled himself with the thought that Beddows would not be there, though the knowledge that he'd killed a man did not rest easily with him. He was certain that as a known criminal, he would gain little sympathy for his plea that he had acted in self defence.

His fears were compounded when, en-route for the farmhouse, he urged his mount to the spot where he had outwitted Beddows, with the thought in his mind that maybe he should bury the body. But, with his horse strangely spooked, he was in for a shock. He sat gazing at the ground where Beddows had been — but all he saw was blank space. He knew he was not mistaken as to the location because there was a colouring of blood on the earth and stones, but as for the body — nothing.

Apprehension, fear, chilled his bones. Either somebody had removed the body, or Beddows had survived.

Frank Miller shuddered.

Greatly dismayed by his discovery, he heeled his horse forward. He didn't know what awaited him at the farmhouse, but he might well be pushing his head into a noose.

An hour later he left the animal tethered in the brush, making certain it was well hidden. Gazing at the sullen buildings, he knew that he must approach with the utmost caution. Beddows might have returned, nursing his sore head and lusting for revenge.

Frank drew his gun and checked that there was a shell beneath the hammer. He circled the house, keeping to the trees, and approached from the rear. Everything seemed silent, apart from the creak of the windmill and the hogs snorting from the pen. They were probably hungry.

He crept up to one of the rear windows and peered inside. The room looked untidy but was deserted. He found a back door, quietly tried it. It was bolted from the inside. Pausing frequently to listen, he crept around the side of the building. He was conscious of the hairs in the nape of his neck tingling and he wondered if, despite his caution, he was being watched. Maybe when he rounded the corner of the house, Beddows would be waiting with a shot gun, ready to blast him into the next world.

He wasn't, and Frank found himself stepping up onto the front porch, cursing as the old boards creaked beneath his boot. The main door still stood open, exactly the same as it had been on his last visit.

He repeated his search of the rooms, moving stealthily, but nothing had changed. No Lucinda, no Beddows.

He found some bread in the kitchen. He tore at it with his teeth, glad of anything to relieve his hunger. Despite his earlier intentions, he was not keen on lingering in this place at all. It seemed that Beddows might still be alive, and, if that was so, he was likely to return at any moment. Perhaps Frank had been foolish to imagine that the house would reveal some clue as to Lucinda's whereabouts.

Grunting with disappointment, he stepped outside. Once again, he became aware of the raucous snorting from the hog-pen. His heart softened towards the hungry beasts. He wasn't too knowledgeable about hogs, but from their noise it seemed that nobody had been around to feed them for some time. He peered into an adjacent barn and spotted a sack of grain. Hoisting it onto his shoulder, he moved to the pen. Looking over the pen-wall, he saw the hogs milling around in the mud. Suddenly his eyes focused on something else. The blackness of a woman's hair.

When he saw the body, nausea rose in him.

At first he tried to imagine his eyes were playing tricks, that he was the centre of some horrific nightmare from which wakefulness would release him. But the doubt crumbled inside him.

He was gazing at the naked body of his wife Lucinda.

11

For a moment the hope danced in him that she might still be alive, that there might yet be some stirring in the body he had once known so intimately. But horror flooded through him. His legs felt like jelly, his chest grew tight and he had to steady himself.

He should never have allowed the differences to arise that had soured their love, that had driven her into the arms of another man. He should never have allowed himself to be cuckolded, never submitted to conviction for a crime he had not committed. He should never . . .

The grunt and snort of the hogs invaded his recriminations. The huge black monsters were prodding her body with their snouts, their tongues lolling as they prepared to feast upon her pale flesh. He roared with anguish. He leaped over the wall of the pen, into the mire within, driving the beasts squealingly away with savage kicks of his booted feet. Stooping, he slipped his arms beneath her, raising her up. Seconds later, he had returned to the outside of the pen, was slumped on the ground, his wife cradled in his arms. There was blood upon her, down her left side, seeping from the twin bullet holes in her shoulder. A short time more, and the hogs would have sunk their teeth into her, mutilated her, eventually consuming her until there was nothing left.

He made no effort to stem the grief, the anger that engulfed him.

He had no doubt who had committed this hideous crime. Beddows had clearly survived to return to his farmhouse, inflict his fury on Lucinda by shooting her, and then tossed her body to the hogs in the belief that they would soon transfer her remains to their bellies, thus destroying all evidence.

But suddenly an incredible thing happened. As Frank cradled his wife's body, he felt movement in her, a stirring of her arms and all at once she groaned. Astonishment had him crying out her name, and at that moment, gazing into her bruised, pain contorted face, he saw her eyelids flutter, then lift from her eyes. He saw terror widen them further, then recognition dawned in her and the terror faded, and in a scarcely audible whisper, she said, 'Ty did it.' Her eyelids descended, for a moment he feared that she had died, but then he became aware of her breathing — firm and steady.

The pound of approaching hoofs intruded into his awareness. He looked up to see a posse of riders approaching and he caught the glint of metal pinned to the foremost rider's chest and knew that the so-called law had arrived.

He groaned. Once they recognized him, they would drag him back to the town jail for onward transmission to the penitentiary. Everything would be lost.

'What's he holdin'?' somebody yelled as they reined in their horses around him.

Then another man exclaimed, 'My God!' and Frank felt he was surrounded by incredulous eyes burning into him. The next words rammed into him like a glowing branding iron. 'It's his wife. He must've killed her for jealousy. Her runnin' off with Beddows an' all!'

Guns had been drawn from holsters, hammers clicked back, muzzles trained on Frank. Anger flared in him.

'She's not dead, damn you,' he shouted. 'We've got to get her to a doctor straight away. Beddows shot her, dumped her in the hog pen. He thought she was dead, that the hogs would eat her. Now get a blanket to wrap around her and hurry about it.'

'Where's Beddows?' a thick-set, beetle-browed man enquired, leaning from his saddle and addressing Frank. He seemed to be the leader of the posse, but he wasn't Marshal Dixon. He was probably his full time deputy.

'He's run off, maybe hidin' out in the woods,' Frank shouted impatiently. 'Now for God's sake hurry up. We've got to get her to a doctor.'

A blanket was produced and wrapped around Lucinda. She was showing more signs of life, and Frank prayed that conveying her back to town would not be too much for her. He held her close in his arms. She seemed so frail, so weightless, yet he knew that her heart was still beating.

Another member of the posse said, 'We better tie Miller up. After all he's an escaped prisoner, and we don't want to chance him runnin' off.'

'I'm not plannin' to run off,' Frank snapped back. 'All that matters is to get my wife to the doctor.'

The beetle-browed deputy nodded. 'He's right. We'll sort him out when we get back to town. Mind you, Frank Miller, we'll have no option but to shoot you down if you try to escape.'

Frank didn't answer, just glared back.

Some of the posse carried out a quick search of the farmhouse but obviously found no evidence. Frank mentioned that his horse was tethered in the trees and a man was sent to fetch it.

Within ten minutes the party was heading back for town, Frank astride the bay, the blanket-shrouded Lucinda in his arms. Guns had been returned to holsters, his fate briefly held in suspense, and all concern had been focused on Lucinda and getting her into the care of a doctor. Even so, there was no guarantee that she would survive.

It was late afternoon when they reached town and folks stood on the sidewalks as the small cavalcade of riders pulled into the street. Apparently, the marshal was away, had gone on some errand to Custer City to see the judge on legal business. He wasn't expected back till next day. Meanwhile, Lucinda's body was consigned to the doctor.

Frank laid her gently on the cot at

the back of the surgery. Doctor Speedwell was a gaunt, towering man in his sixties with a face straight from the scriptures. He lit his Argand lamp, setting it alongside the cot, then he heated some water and bathed Lucinda's wounds, cleansing them with carbolic acid.

'Nasty contusion,' he announced. 'Upper ribs fractured. I'll have to dig those bullets out. It won't be easy.' He gave Frank a glance and added, 'It's a miracle she's survived so far. Can't be sure she'll pull through the surgery, but I'll do my best. Now if you gentlemen would leave me to my work, I'd be obliged. I don't like operating under scrutiny.'

The beetle-browed deputy nodded, and the reluctant Frank was led across the street to the jailhouse.

Only after he had been placed behind bars, did he start protesting his innocence — but he might just as well have hurled words into the wind, for nobody listened to him. He was no

125

stranger to his cell; he had occupied the same accommodation when he had been arrested on the trumped-up charge of cattle theft. Now, the thought that Beddows was still alive brought him no comfort.

He spent that night sprawled on the wooden bunk, sleepless and haunted by thoughts of Lucinda and whether she would still be alive come morning.

He concluded that he attracted trouble like a magnet drew pins. Had he remained in Kansas, even bigamously married Elsa under his assumed identity, he might have escaped discovery and his return here would not have sparked off Lucinda's terrible injuries. Now, it was impossible to determine what would happen though he had the unhealthy feeling that he would get little sympathy from any jury, and the average judge would have no hesitation in returning him to prison.

By the time the first glimmer of dawn was showing through his cell window, he had found no solution to his problems, had been unable to form any sort of plan. But the deputy gave him some relief with the news that the doctor had extracted the bullets from Lucinda, and she was currently sleeping off the sedatives he'd given her.

Frank sighed with relief. It seemed the next milestone in his existence would be the return of Town Marshal Dixon from his business trip.

He was granted a breakfast of greasy pork and bread, washed down with a mug of water. The guard attending him could have been a deaf-mute for he made no response to Frank's protestations, but kept a constant leer on his unshaven face.

Presently, Frank tested the strength of the bars of the window and door and found them solid.

He sat out the hours of the morning, sensing occasional eyes staring in at him, eyes that disappeared whenever he lifted his head. He felt like a caged and dangerous animal, driven crazy by his inability to take any action to improve his situation.

At last, in the early afternoon, there was a buzz of movement in the outer office and voices were raised, and Frank realized that Marshal Dixon had returned. Frank braced himself for what was to happen next.

There was no waiting time. Dixon unlocked the cell, stepped inside, while his deputy hovered on the other side of the bars, gripping a Winchester.

Dixon was a florid man with a tobacco-stained moustache. He had been town marshal for twenty years. Frank was surprised to see that his expression was tolerably pleasant.

'I'm sorry about what happened to your wife, Frank,' he said. 'I'm glad she's pullin' through.'

Frank nodded. 'Beddows did it. She told me. I'm sure he meant to kill her. Maybe he found out that she had begged me to take her away. Maybe he found out that she'd told me that the charge of cattle theft was a put-up trick. I can't say that Lucinda and I were always truly happy but I never figured she'd run off with another man, particularly Beddows. I guess he bullied her into it.'

Dixon was nodding sagely. 'You better tell me your side of the story, Frank.' He sat down beside Frank on the cell bunk. He drew the makings of a cigarette from his pocket, passed them to Frank, then he made one for himself and both men lit up.

Frank spent the next half hour relating how he'd escaped from the penitentiary and gone to Kansas. He made no reference to his change of identity, his inheritance of the Coppinger ranch or his promise to marry Elsa. But he related how he had gone to Beddows' farmhouse and spoken to Lucinda, how she'd told him of her unhappiness — and then how Beddows had turned up, threatened him with a gun, and set out for town with him as a prisoner. Dixon smiled as he explained how he had escaped from the man.

'You should have made sure he was

dead,' he commented surprisingly.

Frank said, 'Lucinda wouldn't have been shot if I'd done the job properly. I could have sworn his skull cracked, but it must've been made of iron instead of bone. Now God knows where he's lurking.'

As he finished relating his experiences, Marshal Dixon made a surprising revelation.

'Frank, there's somethin' you need to know. While Beddows was bringin' you into town, Lucinda rode like the wind, takin' a short cut to town so that she could speak to me before you an' Beddows showed up. She told me everythin' — how she deeply regretted getting involved with him, how foolish she'd been to desert you, how Beddows had hatched up a plan to put you behind bars. She was nigh crazy with remorse.'

Frank gasped with shock.

'When she left, I don't know where she went, but Beddows must've met up with her. Maybe he forced her to tell him what she'd done, maybe they had a row. But the fact is he shot her and tried to dispose of the body in that awful way. When she told me how the charge of cattle theft had been a fixed up job, I rode to Custer City, had a long talk with Judge Sissons. You remember, he was the judge who sentenced you?'

Frank nodded. 'I'll never forget.'

'Well, the judge quashed your sentence on the new evidence. He's issued a reprieve. I've got the certificate, signed by the judge, in my pocket.'

Frank sighed with relief.

Dixon went on. 'I'm issuing a warrant for the arrest of Beddows, so as far as I'm concerned, you're a free man, Frank.'

Frank could hardly believe his ears, but he wasn't going to argue.

★ ★ ★

It had been a month since Frank had left the ranch in Kansas and summer

131

had changed to the fall. During the time after he was cleared of the charge of cattle theft he arranged for Lucinda, when she was well enough, to continue her recuperation with her mother in Custer City where she could be under both maternal and medical care. But he knew it would be a long time before she could resume a normal life.

She had pleaded with him for forgiveness for her infidelity, and he had spoken comforting words. However, deep inside, he questioned himself as to what forgiveness meant. He could never forget what she had done. Could he ever live with it?

Meanwhile he thought seriously about his future. He considered the wisdom of never returning to Kansas, of throwing off the shackles that bound him to the assumed identity of Cyrus Coppinger.

But his job as top foreman of Clancy's Ranch twenty miles from this town, had long been filled by another man. He had nothing here in Clayton.

In Kansas he was a rancher with a healthy bank balance.

Furthermore, the memory of Elsa came to him. She would be anxiously awaiting his return. His feelings for her were troublesome. There was something special about her, something far surpassing the ugliness of the scars on her face. If beauty was only skin deep, so was ugliness. He also felt that he had obligations in Kansas, obligations that were not Cyrus Coppinger's, but were his own, no matter what identity he had taken on.

Here in Wyoming, Ty Beddows had not been apprehended for his crime of attempted murder. He had disappeared; so far as was known, he had never returned to his farm, and his animals had been cared for by a neighbour. Frank guessed that he was biding his time, waiting for a chance to avenge himself on the man he considered had caused his ruination.

That being so, Frank decided that his future lay in Kansas.

So, five weeks to the day after he had returned to Clayton, he bade farewell to Town Marshal Dixon, boarded the train and travelled south. He was cleared of his earlier crimes, but he was still guilty of deception, although he believed that he was the only person aware of it. He was by choice again taking on the mantle of that guilt.

Frank arrived late in the evening at Calico Crossing. As he stepped from the stage, the town was quiet and nobody paid him any attention. He stayed overnight at the Grand Palace Hotel, enjoying a good night's sleep. Next morning he partook a hearty breakfast at *Jake's Café*, then he purchased a horse from the livery and rode out to the Coppinger Ranch. Riding across the range, he wondered what awaited him. There was a brooding silence about the land that seemed almost like a fore-warning. He encountered his own cattle, grazing contentedly enough, but as he approached the familiar ranch house he was beset with trepidation.

He expected that Jim Dodson would be around, but as he reined in his horse, dismounted and stepped up onto the porch, it was his ranch hand, Chet Morgan, who stepped out to meet him.

After they had greeted each other, Frank stepped inside and asked where Dodson was.

Morgan frowned. 'Boss, he quit here soon after you left. Didn't give no reason, but we heard he was working as foreman over at Amundson's spread.'

'Amundson's spread!' Frank gasped in surprise. 'Why should he do that?'

'From what we heard, he struck up some sort of deal with Amundson. There was even some talk that he'd taken a fancy to Elsa Amundson.'

Frank felt as if he'd been kicked in the guts. He could hardly believe his ears. He had trusted Dodson, treated him as a good friend. But the man's affability, apparent sincerity, must have been nothing more than a façade. He'd been acting a part for reasons of his own. Frank had confided in the man and that had been a big mistake. Now, God only knew what would happen.

★ ★ ★

He knew that he had escaped one barrel-full of trouble, only to step into another. Unless he turned tail and disappeared, it was something he had to brave out.

He spent the next week in getting ranch affairs in order. The heat of summer had been replaced by cold winds and the warning of coming winter. His Osage woman Maria kept the house clean and cooked him good food. Chet Morgan had done a fine job in keeping the place ticking over during his absence, but there was still plenty to sort out. All the while Frank was smarting at the thought of Dodson letting him down, and even worse, most likely telling Elsa and her father what he had revealed in confidence.

As the days slipped by, he stayed

away from Calico Crossing, sending Chet Evans on the necessary errands. He guessed Amundson, Elsa and Dodson would be well aware of his return, and he wondered what action was being planned. It was highly unlikely that they would allow matters to rest as they were.

Finally, he could stand the uncertainty no longer, and he decided to ride to Amundson's ranch and find out what was going on. Despite everything that he'd heard, he longed to see Elsa again.

He left early on a Sunday morning, and presently crossed over the dividing fence that separated his range from Amundson's. The skies were leaden, the ranges gaunt, and the gusty wind brought a splattering of rain and he was obliged to put on his yellow slicker. He didn't hurry, but allowed himself time to plan his actions. But few ideas came to him, and the more he pondered the less he understood why things had turned out the way they had.

Just before noon, he reached the rise

overlooking Amundson's ranch. The place appeared prosperous, with the bustle of activity in the sheds and corrals surrounding the big house. As he rode in, he was greeted by the arrogant stares of Amundson's cowhands, but they made no attempt to stop him. Reaching the house, he dismounted and hitched his horse to the rail. Then he stepped up to the porch and rang the hanging bell alongside the big main door.

The door was opened by Elsa herself. Her expression hardened as she recognized Frank, her purple eyes blazing resentment.

'Cyrus Coppinger,' she said, 'you should never have come here!'

'What's happened, Elsa?' he gasped.

For a moment it seemed she was considering slamming the door in his face, but then her father's voice sounded from behind her, and Frank saw Amundson over her shoulder.

'You are not welcome here,' Amundson rapped out. 'Things have got to be sorted out, many things! And you have a lot to account for, Cyrus Coppinger . . . or what ever other name you care to take on!'

Frank felt horrified. For a second he was speechless. What in Heaven's name had Dodson told them?

'Get off my land!' Amundson shouted. 'If you ever show up here again, I will have you shot.'

Frank opened his mouth to speak but no words emerged. He was struck dumb. Under their relentless glare, he returned to his horse and mounted up. He knew that he would discover nothing of the cause for their hostility today.

12

'A girl like you,' Jim Dodson said, as he joined Elsa sitting on the house porch, 'a girl like you with a nasty scar on her face, I mean. Well, you need somebody strong to protect you. I can understand why you've turned against the man you call Cyrus Coppinger. I don't blame you. Agreeing to marry you so's he could get out of jail. That was just downright mean.'

Elsa shot him a questioning glance. She did not like the man. Now she felt the bitterness burning inside her, but something Dodson had said stuck in her mind.

'What do you mean,' she said, 'the man I call Cyrus Coppinger? That's his name, isn't it?'

Dodson cleared his throat awkwardly. He wasn't used to speaking in pussy-foot terms to females, but right now he was anxious to tread carefully.

'Well, Elsa my dear, one day you'll learn the truth, and what you learn will make you thank the good lord that you realized just how wicked the man is.'

'Tell me the whole truth,' she demanded, despite his hesitant manner which seemed so contrary to his true and often bullish character.

'No, Elsa. I can't tell you the whole truth, not yet. I don't want to hurt you more than you've been hurt already.'

She emitted an impatient snort, but he pressed on.

'Like I said, a girl like you needs a protectin' hand . . .'

'Well,' she interrupted, 'if that 'protectin' hand' happens to belong to you, Jim Dodson, then you best keep it to yourself.'

He made a sound akin to a wolf's snarl. 'You'll change your mind, Elsa Amundson. You'll realize you won't get many offers like I'm makin' to you!'

'And I'll thank God for that!'

She rose to her feet in a lithe

movement and strode swiftly into the shadowed interior of the house. She felt in desperate need of getting away from the place, getting away from Dodson's contriving attentions. But at present all she could do was brood on her unhappiness and feel the isolation into which she had been forced. On the fourth day, she packed her bag and left on the morning stage out of Calico Crossing. Thirty miles south, at Wilmot Springs, her Aunt Laura lived. She knew she would be welcome to stay there while she worked out the best thing to do.

★　★　★

The following Friday was pay-day at Amundson's ranch, and apart from Dodson, a Mexican retainer called Roberto Silvado and his wife Francisca, the entire crew went into town on a rowdy binge. That evening, with the ranch almost deserted and unusually silent, Dodson's thoughts continually dwelt on Elsa, or in particular her sensuous body. He grew breathless as he thought of ripping her clothes off, or having his way with her.

He stepped out from the bunkhouse and saw a light burning in the main house. It came from Amundson's office and he was obviously working late on his paperwork. Dodson figured now might be the ideal moment to play his hand.

He walked over to the house, mounted the porch and rang the hanging bell alongside the main door. On the second ring, he heard Amundson call out: 'Come in, whoever's there!'

Having visited the office on frequent occasions, Dodson entered the house and crossed the big room and went into the book-lined, small room that served as the office. Amundson looked up from his desk and gave Dodson a nod. There was no warmth in his greeting. He was angry with Dodson. Over the last two weeks, the man had taken to drinking heavily — and when he did his whole attitude changed, showing a belligerence that he usually kept concealed. It was as if there were two persons inside one body. In fact he'd been seriously considering firing Dodson.

'I thought you would have gone to town with the rest of the crew,' he said, as if he would have welcomed his absence.

Dodson removed his hat, fingering the brim as he chose his words carefully. He smelt of whiskey.

'Mister Amundson, sir,' he said, 'there's somethin' I want to discuss with you, somethin' mighty important.'

'I am busy right now,' Amundson said impatiently.

'This won't wait,' Dodson countered, a flush rising in his face.

Amundson threw his pencil down. 'Speak your mind then.'

Dodson spat his next words out as if they hurt his mouth. 'Mister Amundson, I'd like to ask for the hand of your daughter in marriage. She needs a strong man to look after her.'

Amundson's lower lip dropped in surprise. 'That wouldn't be part of my plan. I have been thinking hard. Maybe I was too harsh on Coppinger. I still hope things will get patched up between him and Elsa. If you had not talked, there would have been no trouble.'

Dodson forced a grin on to his face, but it wasn't the friendly grin he so often assumed. 'I know why you're so set on gettin' so-called Cyrus Coppinger to marry Elsa,' he said. 'It's because you think that once they're wed, in the event of anything happenin' to him, which maybe you'd arrange, the Coppinger land would be inherited by Elsa and you'd be able to get your hands on it.'

'That is a lie!' Amundson stormed, thumping his fist on his desk. His eyes darted towards the six-shooter on the side table, but Dodson sensed his intention.

'Don't try any daft tricks,' he snarled,

his eyes widening. 'You just listen to what I got to say. Listen, damn you!'

Amundson's gaze sparked with hatred, but he slumped back. He reckoned that Dodson could gun him down in a flash if he attempted grabbing his own weapon.

Dodson said, 'You're wastin' your time, plannin' things for the man you call Cyrus Coppinger.'

'What d'you mean the man I call Cyrus Coppinger?' Amundson demanded

'He's not Cyrus Coppinger.'

Amundson started to speak, but then paused as Dodson's words sank in.

'What you are saying is madness,' he said.

'But it's true, even so,' Dodson retorted. 'And I'll tell you how I know.'

'How?'

'Because *I'm* Cyrus Coppinger,' Dodson said. 'I'm Old John Coppinger's nephew.'

Amundson's mouth fell open.

Dodson glared at him. 'Can't your dim mind recognize the truth when you hear it. If you want to know, six months back I got drunk and lost the legal documents in a poker game to some sick-looking fellow. I've been tryin' to track him down ever since. I don't know how the man pretendin' to be me got hold of those documents. Maybe he stole them. However, I figure they're rightfully mine, seein' I was not my sober self when I lost them.'

'That fellow's posing as you!' Amundson exclaimed. He made a visible effort to control himself, his next words coming slowly as he came to terms with what the other man had said. 'Why have you not spoken up before now, then?'

Dodson emitted a heavy sigh. 'Me and you have got to draw up plans. It's not easy, but we have to come to . . . an arrangement. In that way you can get possession of the Coppinger range and ranch, and I can get compensation for what's rightly mine.'

Amundson swallowed hard. 'Why can't you come out and prove your identity, if what you tell me is true?'

'I don't make a habit of spreadin' this around,' Dodson muttered, 'but there are certain people, mainly the town marshal, who know that it was me who killed my uncle.'

'Killed Old John Coppinger!' Amundson gasped. 'You! Why would you kill your own uncle?'

'I got word he was gonna change his will, gonna remarry you-know-who. That's when I sensed what you were up to. He intended to cut off my inheritance. So I paid him a visit. I slipped onto the ranch when he was alone. It was just like you and me now. Only he was downright unreasonable, drew a gun on me, so . . .'

'You murdered him!' Amundson cut in.

'Self defence — but Marshal Rainbird won't believe that. He was friendly with the Old Man.'

'So Marshal Rainbird knows that the fella runnin' the Coppinger ranch is not Cyrus Coppinger?'

Dodson nodded. 'I guess he's bidin' his time until he can track down the real Cyrus Coppinger. He doesn't know it's me, and I don't aim in advertisin' my identity, not yet for a while, anyway. That's why you and me've got to draw up a plan. First thing I want from you is an agreement for Elsa and me to get married. She's an ugly bitch and you should be glad that some man is prepared to take her on. By that way, you'll be takin' the first steps to get your hands on the Coppinger land.'

Amundson didn't look up. He was breathing heavily, seemed to have shrivelled into himself, as if he'd aged thirty years.

'You hear what I say?' Dodson demanded.

'I was a fool to take you on, with your friendly ways,' Amundson said. 'You hoodwinked me. I should have seen what you really were. As for what you're suggesting . . .'

The Norwegian raised his eyes and

his words came with the impact of a snake's venom.

'*Cyrus Coppinger, or whoever the hell you are, I would rather do business with the Devil!*'

Then, knowing he was dicing with death, he snatched up his gun from the side table.

★ ★ ★

At just after eight the next morning, Deputy Town Marshal Andy Mac-Donald was opening up his office when the pound of hoofs in the street had him turning. Amundson's Mexican retainer Roberto Silvano half fell from the back of his sweat-cached animal, his sombrero blown from his head and trailing by the cord, his face wreathed in anguish.

'Marshal, sir,' he panted out, 'it's *Señor* Amundson! Him . . . dead!'

'Dead!' the surprised lawman gasped.

'Sure . . . shot dead. I see it with my own eyes.'

150

The deputy marshal tried to steady his stunned senses. A crowd was forming around them, drawn by the agitation.

'I see it with my own eyes,' the Mexican repeated. 'Cyrus Coppinger did the shootin'. Nigh blew a hole in poor *Señor* Amundson's chest. I think they had some argument over his daughter.'

'Well I guess we should find Coppinger,' somebody yelled. 'String him up.'

'There'll be no lynch law here,' Deputy Marshal MacDonald shouted. 'Any guilty party'll get a fair trial.'

'If that's the case,' another man shouted, 'why are we standin' here. Swear us in as deputies and we'll ride out and bring the murderer in.'

And a dozen or more men were shouting agreement.

As MacDonald went through the quick swearing in ceremony, he felt decidedly uneasy. If his posse set their minds on a hanging, there was little he

151

or anybody else could do to stop them tossing a loop over the nearest tree and stringing a man up. Amundson had never been a popular member of the community, but now you'd have figured he was the best loved fellow in the entire territory by the way this mob were howling for retribution.

Fifteen minutes later the posse was mounted, armed and heading for the Coppinger ranch.

Roberto Silvano, the Mexican retainer stood alone in the street, forgotten by all. Unknowingly, he had told the truth when he had claimed that Cyrus Coppinger had killed Amundson — but he had acted under threat. The man he knew as Dodson had gunned Amundson down. Amundson had stood no chance once he had decided on gunplay.

And Roberto, too, had feared for his life when Dodson realized that he had witnessed the killing. But it wasn't towards Roberto that Dodson raised his threat. It was towards the

Mexican's wife and baby.

'You go to town,' Dodson had ordered Roberto. 'You spread word that Cyrus Coppinger, from the Coppinger ranch, killed Amundson and you saw it happen. Cold blooded murder! You tell the marshal that or your wife and daughter will suffer, I promise.'

'Do not hurt them, *Señor!*' the Mexican shrieked, but as his eyes locked with Dodson's cruel orbs, he threw up his hands in despair. '*Si, si, Señor*. I will do what you want. Do not harm them. I promise I will do what you want!'

★ ★ ★

Deputy Marshal Andy MacDonald felt desperate as he saw the emotions rising in his hard riding posse. He wished his boss, Marshal Aaron Rainbird, hadn't been off-duty. Yesterday, the veteran lawman had visited his sick sister over at Buller's Fork. He'd got back late and was sleeping in this morning with his

153

long-term girl-friend Lily Lovall. But MacDonald sent him a note, saying what was happening.

Old John Coppinger had always been unpopular in town. Some of his dealings had been decidedly unscrupulous, and bitterness against him had been running high. Now that he was dead, most of the posse saw the punishment of his nephew, or the man they thought was his nephew, as a means of payback against the old man. The fact that he was in his grave seemed to be of no consequence.

The riders maintained their hammering pace until they reached Coppinger Ranch. They at last reined-in their horses to take a welcome breather. It was just past noon, the smell of winter was in the air, but both men and animals were sweating.

'Good day for a lynchin',' Brandon Wilkes muttered, and a dozen other throats grunted agreement. Wilkes was a burly individual, known for hitting the bottle hard. He was the loud-mouthed, self-acclaimed leader of the rowdy element in Calico Crossing.

'Hold on,' Andy MacDonald cut in. 'We ain't gonna do nothin' unlawful,' but, being outnumbered by Wilkes's rowdies, he sensed the odds were against him.

The ranch and surrounding spread looked quiet. As they heeled their horses down towards the house, the deputy marshal harboured the vague hope that the man they were hunting might not be at home. He did not know why, but he had always had a soft spot for Cyrus Coppinger, had never believed that he would kill another man in cold blood

The sixteen riders now approached the porch of the house in a line that undulated like a sidewinder, and once again reined-in. Brandon Wilkes rode beside MacDonald, as if anxious to take over leadership of the party, but the deputy would not give way.

'Cyrus Coppinger,' he called out, 'come outside. We want to speak with you.'

Frank Miller had a surprise for the party. Ever since they had entered his ranch yard, he had been watching them from the shadowy interior of his barn. Now he stepped out into the daylight, unarmed, and spoke up in a firm voice. 'I'm listening. Do your talking.'

13

All the riders twisted in their saddles to view him. Brandon Wilkes immediately drew his six-gun and waved it airily, but before he could speak, Andy MacDonald said, 'You've been accused of murderin' Amundson. We're takin' you in to stand trial.'

Frank grunted with shock. Amundson dead . . . he couldn't believe it.

'Murdering Amundson!' he gasped. 'Why, that's crazy! I never . . . '

'I say string him up now,' Brandon Wilkes interrupted, and another man had lifted his coiled rope from his saddle horn.

'Plenty o' trees round here for the job,' Wilkes shouted.

'Like I said,' MacDonald snapped out. 'There'll be no hangin'. We're takin' him in for a fair trial.'

'I think not!' Wilkes yelled, swinging

his gun towards the deputy marshal.

Frank knew he was helpless — just as MacDonald was. Chet Evans was away. The Osage woman Maria was somewhere at the back of the house. He was at the mercy of this blood-hungry crowd, and all he had to defend himself were his fists or maybe the hay-fork leaning against the barn wall.

'This is crazy,' he shouted, but his voice was drowned out by the mob.

In their eyes he could see an unmistakable kill-lust. It blinded them to sanity, settling over them like a fever that could only be assuaged by a man's death — his own!

Deputy MacDonald now showed courage, dragging his pistol from its holster and sending a shot blazing into the sky. His action brought a momentary pause to the surging mob, but Brandon Wilkes was in no mood to be thwarted. He swung his own gun and fired a shot that nicked the lawman's shoulder, sent him spinning around, his weapon dropping from his fingers.

Blood stained his hand as he clutched his wound.

When MacDonald spoke, his words came in a tremble of fury. 'Brandon Wilkes, you'll pay for what you've done today, I swear it.'

Wilkes emitted a scornful laugh and ordered that the rope be tossed over a limb of the tall oak tree that stood at the edge of the yard.

Frank had watched, transfixed to the spot by the sheer horror of the scene unfolding before him. Suddenly he snapped into action, grabbing up the pitchfork.

As the posse surged forward, he swung the vicious implement in a sweeping arc, its sharp tines glinting a lethal warning in the wintry sun, driving the foremost man back with blood seeping through his shirt. His reaction was to wrench his pistol from its leather. He was thumbing back the hammer, when a shot blasted off, but it didn't come from the expected direction. Instead, all eyes swung to the rider who had suddenly appeared in the yard, his weapon still showing a wisp of smoke.

It was Aaron Rainbird, Town Marshal, unmistakable with his bright red bandanna. He was hunched threateningly in the saddle, with a determined look in his wizened eyes.

'Stand away from Coppinger,' he shouted. 'Holster your guns before any more mischief happens!'

A degree of common sense at last seemed to descend on the assembly. Guns slipped back into their leather. Even Wilkes submitted, though with a sour curse.

Deputy MacDonald stooped and retrieved his gun, still nursing his bloody shoulder.

'Thanks, Aaron,' he grunted. 'You sure turned up at the right moment.'

Frank Miller agreed wholeheartedly. He wasn't overfond of staring death so closely in the face.

'Drop the hay-fork, Coppinger,' the marshal ordered. 'I'm takin' you in on a suspicion of killin' Amundson. You'll get a fair trial. If you're innocent, you'll have to prove it.'

Frank hesitated, then threw down the hay-fork.

'I'm grateful to you, Marshal Rainbird,' Frank said. 'If you hadn't showed up, I'd probably be dead by now.' He swung back to the other men. 'The fact is, I haven't seen Amundson for days. I have no reason to kill him. I'm downright sickened to hear what's happened.'

Wilkes was fuming at his humiliation. 'The jury will have to decide whether you're guilty or not. You may have escaped the rope today, but you won't escape no second time!'

The rest of the posse was standing around, all looking shamefaced.

'And Brandon Wilkes,' Marshal Rainbird said, 'you'll face the same jury, charged with woundin' an officer of the law.'

* * *

Within three hours, Frank Miller had once again been locked in the claustrophobic atmosphere of the town jail. He took no satisfaction from the knowledge that the foul mouthed Brandon Wilkes occupied the next cell, bitterly complaining that his gun had gone off by accident, that he had never intended harm on the deputy marshal. MacDonald himself had departed to get his wound attended to by Doctor Newcombe, which left Marshal Rainbird in charge of the prisoners. Despite having saved Frank's life, the marshal now showed him no favours, conducting his duties in a businesslike and monosyllabic manner.

Lifting himself to his barred window, Frank gazed out into the side alley, the view with which he had become so familiar during his previous incarceration. Now it seemed he was back in the same predicament. The irony was that he was being charged with the killing of the man who had previously saved him. He wondered how Elsa would react to the death of her father. The more he thought about it, the stranger it seemed that a father would wish to marry his daughter off to a man he hardly knew, a man accused of murder. Had it just been a ruse for Amundson to get his hands on the Coppinger land? Or were there other reasons? Perhaps Elsa herself had the answers. Was she the innocent, slightly naïve and sweet girl she appeared?

And who had killed her father? It couldn't have been Dodson because he'd been as thick as thieves with Amundson. But then Frank recalled that Dodson had been really friendly towards *him*, so much so that Frank had foolishly confided his secrets to the man, and thus made a huge mistake.

He concluded that Dodson was the root of many of the evils that surrounded him. One thing was certain: secured behind bars, Frank had little chance of finding the answers to the mysteries that plagued him. If he could somehow break free of this damned jail he'd face Dodson and get the truth out of him — or so he reasoned.

He slumped back on the cell bunk, listening to the ravings of Brandon Wilkes from the next cell. He was muttering over and over that his pals wouldn't stand for him being locked up, that the marshal and deputy would pay for what they were doing — and as the hours ticked away, Frank couldn't help worrying that there might be some truth in the man's ramblings. If the jail was overwhelmed by a crowd of rowdies and Wilkes was busted free, they were bound to turn their attention on Frank himself, most likely with intent to complete the lynching they'd been thwarted in out at the ranch.

Frank sighed deeply, lay back on the hard bunk and tried to get some sleep, but Elsa kept probing into his mind and the thought that she might well be in some danger. He felt really bad about her, about the wicked thoughts concerning him that had been planted in her mind. Of course it had been a crazy idea of her father, giving him little alternative but to agree to marry her. At that time he had not realized how his feelings would develop towards the girl.

By nightfall, Wilkes's ramblings had ceased and there had been periods when his snoring had sounded. As darkness took hold, it got cold. The bandaged Andy MacDonald reappeared and served the prisoners food and a jug of water, passing the refreshments through the bars. The deputy didn't seem in any great shape. Apparently, he had lost a lot of blood and the doctor had advised him to take to his bed for a couple of days. But being conscientious, he had decided to resume his duties.

After the meal, things went quiet at the jailhouse. Even Wilkes seemed to have given up snoring, and Frank felt sure he was awake. Maybe he was waiting for something to happen. Maybe this quiet was a lull before a storm.

★ ★ ★

Marshal Rainbird grumbled at Andy MacDonald for not taking time off as the doctor had advised. But the deputy was adamant that he did not need to rest and said that he would take a quiet stroll around town to ensure everything was peaceful. Part of the deputy's patrol took in *The Prairie Belle Saloon*. There, the proprietor told him that he had overheard a crowd of Brandon Wilkes's friends talking about how they intended busting their pal out of jail during the night.

When MacDonald returned to the jailhouse, just before midnight, Marshal Rainbird said, 'Better get barricaded in. We'll most likely have to defend ourselves against them drunken devils.'

'I'll see to it,' Andy MacDonald responded. 'You keep watch from the window. I'll get the doors bolted and drag the desk across. Anyway, maybe it was just drunken talk.'

'I don't think so,' Rainbird responded.

After MacDonald had dragged some of the furniture around to form protection, Frank heard the sound of guns being lifted down from the wall rack and loaded in readiness.

The lawmen weren't taking any chances, but Frank had the unhealthy feeling that sheer force of numbers would overwhelm them, and he himself was helpless to do anything but wait to see what happened. Could it be that before dawn, he would be dangling on the end of a rope and all his struggling, his reasoning, would be wasted?

As for Wilkes, he'd gone downright quiet. He'd heard the lawmen talking, just as Frank had, and was probably now sitting back on his bunk, a smug smile on his face as the big hand on the office clock inched the minutes away.

It was just after one o'clock that night when events took their nightmare turn.

Frank had not bothered with sleep, feeling tense and anxious about what might happen. Suddenly the faintest sounds, coming from the street beyond his barred window, alerted him. It was the almost inaudible dislodgement of a pebble, but it was enough to have him rolling off his bunk and seeking cover beneath it. Simultaneously a thunderous roar shook the cell, the thump of a bullet splintering the wood of the bunk coupled with the brief flash of a gunshot.

Frank was aware that the barrel of a rifle had been thrust through his prison window. The heavy-calibre bullet would have smashed into the body of anybody sprawled on the bunk, offering no chance of survival.

As it was, Frank felt a great shudder go through him. He had escaped death by the narrowest of margins, and not for the first time. How long could his luck last?

The resonance of the gun blast subsided into his ears, and he could hear other sounds. The alarmed shouting of the lawmen from the outer office, and other voices sounding from the street fronting the building.

One voice rose above the rest, clear and threatening.

'Marshal, you set Brandon Wilkes free and hand over that other scum you've got locked up and there'll be no more trouble!'

Frank remained beneath his wooden cover, until he was sure that whoever had attempted to kill him was gone. He was aware that all light had been extinguished in the office, but he could hear the hushed murmurings of the two lawmen, although he couldn't catch what they were saying.

Then the voice from outside sounded again, and there was nothing hushed about its grim warning. 'You got five minutes to hand over them prisoners. If you don't, we'll bust in and grab 'em for ourselves. Then we'll torch the whole place. With ineffective law in the town, we've formed a vigilante committee.'

Now it was Marshal Rainbird's answer that bludgeoned into the night. 'Me and Deputy MacDonald are the duly elected peace officers of this town, directly responsible to the County Sheriff. If you break the law tonight, you'll pay for it, every one of you!'

There was a pause, then a volley of gunfire sounded and there was the tinkling of shattered glass.

Frank felt sweat beading out on his forehead and cursed his helplessness. He'd stand no chance if the lawmen were overwhelmed, and he was suddenly aware of the danger of somebody coming up the side street and firing through the cell window again — but his thoughts were interrupted as a white-faced Andy MacDonald appeared at his cell door and slipped a key into the lock. The door swung open.

'In case you need to defend yourself,' he said, 'you better have this. There's five shots in the chamber. But remember you're still a prisoner. It won't do you no good to play any tricks.'

Frank grasped the six-gun gratefully, nodding his thanks.

At that moment Brandon Wilkes

called out from his cell. 'How about me? I need a gun too!'

MacDonald's response came tersely. 'Go to hell, Wilkes. Those are your buddies outside. They won't harm you unless they mistake you for somebody else.'

Wilkes swore. 'If they set fire to this place, I'll be trapped like a turkey in an oven.'

When no further response came, he lapsed into silence.

Plenty of noise was coming from the street. It seemed a sizeable mob was gathered. They were armed with guns, rocks and bottles and were shouting for the prisoners to be handed over. A number of them had ignited torches, and the light from these flickered through the office, casting a weird glow over everything. In this Frank could see the two lawmen, crouching close to the windows, their weapons drawn. The white of the deputy's bandage indicated how handicapped he was.

As Frank joined them, a voice from

outside rose above the others. 'We gave you five minutes to hand over them prisoners, marshal. You ain't done it, so you must accept the consequences and . . .'

The final words were drowned out by the shouted agreement of the mob.

14

'What are we gonna do?' Andy MacDonald gasped.

The two lawmen's faces showed as orange tinted smudges in the gloom.

Frank, crouching beside them, could see the seething mass of humanity beyond the porch step outside — a sea of angry faces. The street was filled with movement, the flame of torches giving the scene a ghostly ambience.

Frank took a deep breath, then said, 'The main reason they're so riled up is because of me. If I was out of here, the whole affair would fizzle out. Best thing you could do would be to let Wilkes go, and arrest him later when it suits you. The charge'll still stand, and a few more as well.'

'No chance,' Andy MacDonald muttered. 'You're under arrest as well, and we don't give up prisoners without a fight.'

'I tell you,' Frank countered, 'I did not kill Amundson. I was nowhere near his place at the time.'

MacDonald started to argue again, but Marshal Rainbird cut across him.

'Let's hear what he's suggestin'.'

'I'm suggesting that I get out o' here, somehow through the back way. If I can escape, I can ride to Milton City and bring in the county sheriff to help out. If you pretend to give in to this mob, the wind will be taken out of their sails when they find I'm not here. And I'll give you my word on one thing.'

'What's that?'

'I'll turn myself over to you after things have settled down.'

'You won't stand a chance o' getting clear o' this place,' Andy MacDonald muttered, but his final words were drowned out by the increased shouting from outside.

Marshal Rainbird made a sudden decision. 'OK, I guess it's our only chance. Go now, and I hope you get away!'

Frank paused only to nod his head, then he backed towards the rear of the office, finding the only window shuttered from the inside. He slid the bolts back on the shutter, praying that there was nobody waiting outside. In desperate haste he forced up the sash window and lifted his legs over the sill, dropping down into the shadowy scrub and weeds, ignoring the stab of thorns into his flesh. Head down, he forced his way through tall grass believing that any sound he made would be drowned out by the racket going on from the front of the building. But he was wrong because somebody called out, 'Is that you, Johnson?' And before he knew it, he had blundered into the solid figure of a man, sending him tumbling back. Frank didn't delay to find out who he'd encountered. He staggered, regained his balance and struggled on. When he finally paused to regain his breath, he could hear a great commotion coming from the jail-house. He hoped that his prediction that the mob would lose interest once they had released Wilkes and discovered that Frank, himself, was no longer there, would prove correct — but now was not the time to find out.

By twenty minutes later, he was clear of the town, climbing through the forest that rose to the east. He had promised that he would get word to the County Sheriff in Milton City, but to do that he needed a horse. He realised that he was within a few miles of his friend, Fred Starret. He'd bought horses from him in the past. He lived at a small settlement called Pesky Gulch about ten miles east of town. He whispered a quick prayer that the man was at home, then set out towards his place, running as much as he could.

Dawn was tinting the eastern sky as he reached his destination. His hammering knock roused the sixty-year-old Fred Starret, who after a lengthy pause opened the door, gun first. 'Who the hell?' Then, suddenly, enlightenment showed in his eyes and the gun was lowered. 'Why, Cyrus, what's wrong?'

Soon Frank had given him a brief outline of events and Fred Starret, still in his long-johns, was nodding his grizzled head. 'Never did like that fella Wilkes. But you say you've been accused of killin' Amundson.'

'Well, I didn't do it,' Frank said.

Fred Starret said, 'I believe you, but what can I do to help?'

'Let me have a horse. I need to ride to Milton City to alert the county sheriff. The sooner he gets to Calico Crossing the better. I just hope it won't be too late.'

'You look tuckered, Cyrus,' Starret said. 'I got a better idea. You get some rest. I'll ride for Milton City, get word to the sheriff. When you've rested, you can borrow one o' my other horses and head for wherever you think fit.'

Frank hesitated, then nodded, glad that he'd sought help from this man.

'I'm sure grateful to you, Fred,' he said.

★ ★ ★

True to his word, Fred Starret appreciated the gravity of the situation in Calico Crossing, forewent the remainder of his night's sleep and set out for Milton City with utmost haste, leaving Frank at his homestead.

The tension of recent events had left Frank weary, and he snatched three hours sleep on Starret's sofa. He awoke imagining he heard voices from outside, but it proved to be the raucous cawing of crows from the nearby trees. However the sound somehow reminded him that he was still in danger.

His mind swung to Elsa. He didn't know where she was. She might be back at the Amundson ranch by now, and Dodson was just as likely to vent his foul anger on her as anybody else.

For a moment he debated whether or not to return to his own ranch, but decided if Brandon Wilkes and his cronies wished to ease their frustrations, they would come hunting for him. And the first place they would look was his ranch. Therefore he decided to head for the Amundson place and at least find out what was going on there.

Fred Starret had offered him the full facility of his larder, so he grabbed some ham and a large slice of molasses pie, washed down with coffee. He went outside and selected a big roan horse from the corral, borrowed some gear from the barn, and saddled the animal. Then he left.

He pushed his mount hard through the cold afternoon, all the while conscious that he was still a wanted man — if not by the marshal himself, then by other less scrupulous men. There was something else that was on his mind. He had promised to turn himself into the marshal once things had settled down, and he intended to keep his word. But firstly there were matters he had to resolve.

He was on the Amundson range by evening and in sight of the ranch house as dusk was yet again taking hold. Several lights glowed from the building. He reined in the lathered roan, considered his options, then went forward at a cautious walk, apprehension rising in him as to what awaited. There was a marked inactivity amid the outbuildings, apart from the plume of smoke that lifted from the bunkhouse chimney. As he came level with some corral fences, he halted the roan, dismounted and hitched the animal to the railing. He walked forward, had stepped up onto the porch when suddenly a tall, big breasted woman appeared in the main-doorway, her eyes widening in alarm as she saw him. She was clearly Mexican and she immediately turned and called out, 'Roberto!'

A moment later her weary looking husband was beside her. His face registered alarm as he saw Frank.

'*Señor*, I thought you were in

jail . . . ' he gasped.

Frank saw little point in prevaricating. 'Well, I escaped. The jail was under siege by that mob of so-called vigilantes. I just hope the marshal has sorted things out by now.'

The Mexican woman was standing hands on her hips, looking somewhat formidable. 'The man Dodson,' she said, 'he force Roberto to go into town and tell the law that you killed *Señor* Amundson. He said if Roberto didn't do like he said, me and the baby would suffer. I am angry that Roberto went into town and told those lies. It was not right. I can look after myself. I've told Roberto that we must go back to town and tell the truth, that it was Dodson who murdered poor *Señor* Amundson. We have buried him in the pasture beyond the corral. I just don't know what Elsa will think, when she comes home and finds her papa in his grave.'

As the woman spoke, her husband was nodding his head. 'It is true what Francisca says, I am sorry I told lies

181

about you, but I was worried about her and the babe.' He gave Frank a look as if seeking his understanding. 'I have taken the babe to my friend, a milk mother, who lives down the valley, so as to be away from any trouble. Now, we must go to town and I will tell the marshal the truth.'

It was Frank's turn to nod. 'I only hope Marshal Rainbird has restored order in town.'

Within ten minutes, Frank, Roberto and his wife Francisca were on their way towards town, galloping through the darkness. The Mexican woman was strong; she rode astride, a shawl about her shoulders, her skirts drawn up and her dark hair streaming out behind her. As they progressed, the moon appeared, painting the surrounding range a ghostly silver.

Frank again wondered what had occurred since his escape from the jail. Again, he hoped that his absence would have caused the vigilantes to simmer down, particularly after Wilkes had been released. And then his mind swung to Elsa. Roberto informed him that she had gone to visit her aunt, but he did not know when she was due to return.

After three hours of riding, punctuated by only brief stops to rest the horses, they reached the rise overlooking the town, and Frank knew that they would have to be careful. They reined in their mounts and gazed down at the town. In the small hours of the night, Cedar Crossing looked quiet and there were no lights showing. The glistening of the river showed from beyond the town, reflecting the cold moon.

After discussion, it was decided that Roberto would ride down to the sheriff's office and inform the law that he'd been forced to lie when he had reported the killing of Amundson. Frank was again aware that he had promised to turn himself in once the trouble had subsided. Once his innocence was confirmed, it would make things much easier. Consequently Roberto left Frank and Francisca amid some shadowy rocks.

Frank and Francisca dismounted, stiff and chilled after being in the saddle for so long. Impatiently, they waited as the minutes dragged by. It was only five days ago that Francisca had given birth to her daughter. She was a strong woman, an Amazon, and Frank admired her.

For a while, Roberto's white-clad figure showed, illuminated by the stars, but eventually, on reaching the outskirts of town, he disappeared. Francisca kept watch, deeply concerned for the safety of her husband.

'He is sick,' she murmured. 'His chest is not good. All this trouble has been a big strain for him.'

For what seemed an eternity, they waited, their eyes aching with the constant watch on the town down the slope. There was still no sign of activity or life from the shadowy buildings. Eventually the stars were gone and the pre-dawn was taking hold, streaking the eastern horizon with a thin line of pink. Poor-wills began their repetitious calls from the nearby pine trees.

'I hope there will be no more trouble,' Francisca said. 'Too many people have died already.'

'They sure have,' Frank agreed.

'It was terrible when *Señor* Coppinger died,' the Mexican woman continued. 'The blood was pouring out of him, and there was nothing I could do. He died in my arms.'

Frank was surprised. 'I didn't realize you knew him.'

'Oh yes. I used to work for him. He was so good to me. Just like a father to me. I loved him. When he died he told me that Cyrus Coppinger had shot him.'

'I didn't do it,' Frank said.

'I know that now,' she said. 'But I do not understand it. Perhaps there are two Cyrus Coppingers.'

Frank didn't comment. He didn't know what to say.

'I could see trouble ahead,' she said. 'It was not right that *Señor* Coppinger should marry again.'

'Marry?' Frank queried.

'*Sí*, I thought you knew.'

'No,' he said, his interest quickening.

'She was so much younger than he was. I do not think she loved him, but she had her reasons.'

'Reasons? Who was she?'

Francisca turned to face him, then she spoke the name that shook him to the roots of his being.

'Elsa Amundson. I thought you knew.'

Frank felt stunned.

Suddenly Francisca's attention was distracted. 'Look, Roberto is coming.'

Glancing down the slope, Frank spotted movement, and this rapidly materialized into the Mexican's white-clad figure. He was forcing his horse up the slope at a brisk pace. He seemed to have miscalculated their position, for he reached them still riding hard, but he immediately drew rein and swung back.

One look at his face told Frank that he had bad news.

'Terrible things have happened,' he panted out. 'Marshal Rainbird and his deputy have been killed. Brandon Wilkes has been busted out of jail and the vigilantes have taken control of the town.'

'Oh God!' Frank gasped with horror. 'You must be wrong, Roberto.'

'No, *Señor*,' the Mexican responded. 'It is true. I speak with a friend who works at the blacksmith's. He tell me. He does not lie.'

Frank slumped forward with dismay. He had never suspected that the two lawmen would be killed by the vigilantes. A great remorse swept over him. He blamed himself. In a way, they'd died for him. They hadn't exactly been friends of his, but he knew they had striven to represent justice as they saw it, and their deaths left him heavy hearted.

15

Frank's brain was reeling from the shock of events. When he glanced at the Mexican couple, Francisca said, 'There is nothing more we can do here. We must get back to the baby.'

'*Sí*,' her husband nodded.

Frank and Francisca mounted their horses, and about them the new day was taking hold, the sun rising to flood the land with light. From down in Calico Crossing, a cockerel was crowing lustily, and movement showed along the street. With the night no longer concealing them, Frank felt decidedly vulnerable. He wondered if Fred Starret had made it to Milton City, and if he had, how long it would be before the county sheriff showed up. Alternatively, had the sheriff been away on some other business, or had he been unable to raise a posse? He had obviously been delayed by something. There could be many reasons for this, but with things in their current state, the vicinity of Calico Crossing was an unhealthy place for Frank to linger. He felt he should return to the Coppinger ranch and see if there had been any developments there — but he would have to be wary in case Wilkes and his vigilantes came searching for him.

Roberto and Francisca were intent on retrieving the baby from their friend and then returning to the Amundson spread, so they parted company, each wishing the other good fortune.

Alone now, Frank rode through the morning, catching the first flurry of snow. He did not push his roan too hard for it was weary from the long miles already covered. He paused whenever he came to a stream, to refresh both himself and the horse. Soon the streams would be iced over. His brain was active, trying to reason out his best course of action and hoping that no further disasters awaited him.

With Dodson still at large, there was no telling what evil deeds had been committed. At the Coppinger ranch, he had left the Osage woman Maria and he hoped she had not been molested.

It was just after noon when he saw the smudge of smoke in the blue sky and apprehension cut through him, had him heeling his flagging beast for greater speed. As he drew close, his worst fears were realized. Acrid smoke thickened the air and it was obvious that there had been a considerable fire. The ranch-house at last showed. From it, and the adjacent barn, flames reached skyward in long red streaks and billows of smoke were pouring from the doors and windows.

He reached the barn and half fell from his horse. He plunged inside and was immediately engulfed with smoke. The hay in the loft was ablaze and flame was licking greedily up the back wall. The horses were panicking in their stalls, whinnying in terror, kicking their slats out. He felt deafened by the roar of the fire and the threshing of the animals. Coughing in the acrid smoke, he clawed open the first gate and managed to drag one of his wagon team out of its stall, striving to avoid its slashing hoofs. He slapped the beast's rump and it galloped for the open door. Feeling the scorch of heat, he opened the other stalls and the horses stampeded past him, forcing him to press himself against the stall to avoid being trampled.

He followed them outside, gasping at the sight of the conflagration. The main house was ablaze, so were the outhouses. He guessed the hogs had been burned to death in their pens. And the servant woman Maria?

He rushed towards the house, as near as he dared, his dismayed gaze lingered on the mass of blazing timber and ash that had once been such a fine house. He had spent many hours painting and refurbishing the place, now all his work meant nothing. Tears were streaming down his cheeks, both from anguish and the smoke.

As he watched, a burning rafter collapsed, igniting more timbers. A great burst of flame exploded in an awesome flash, shooting through the billowing smoke. Charred shingles and lengths of wood were cascading down. He heard the shriek of yielding timbers and knew that the entire back wall was collapsing. The upper floor followed, causing the earth to tremble beneath his feet and showering him with sparks. Soon, everything was obscured by sooty clouds.

The heat was torturous, driving him back. His eyes were stinging; he felt blinded. The smoke choked him, burning his lungs and he was overwhelmed by a bout of coughing. The roar of collapsing walls was like thunder.

The house and outbuildings must have been meticulously torched with no thought given to anybody who might have been inside. Nobody, he felt certain, could have survived the inferno.

Please God, he thought, *may Maria have escaped before the flames caught her.*

How could anyone have committed this awful sin?

Despairing, he retreated to a safe distance, knowing that there was nothing he could do. The fire would have to burn itself out.

It was as he recovered that a distant flurry of movement caught his attention. On the hill to the east, he noticed the swift movement of a horse and rider, disappearing as smoke blurred Frank's vision — and one name plunged into his mind like a knife.

Dodson!

Frank unleashed an anguished growl.

Hatred rose inside him like a hard, black stone. The man deserved to die. No human being was worthy of survival, having committed such wickedness!

Frank ran to his spooked roan, calmed the animal and climbed into the saddle. He was glad he still possessed the gun that poor Andy MacDonald had given him. Five shots were in the chamber and he was determined to make them count. He heeled his horse into motion, the beast needing little encouragement to escape the hot, stifling atmosphere of the burning ranch.

He rode towards the east, the smoke gradually clearing around him until he was again given an unhampered view of the distance. The rider had long disappeared, but he'd obviously been following the cattle trail that climbed eastward towards the edge of the Coppinger range. Beyond, lay undulating badlands.

He tried to work out the reasoning of Dodson's insane mind. Maybe he realized that Amundson's murder would eventually be traced to him and it was in his interest to disappear into country so wild that any pursuit would trail off. But he'd been unable to resist the opportunity for one, final blow to destroy Frank. Fire was the obvious means of ruining everything that had been built up with such painstaking care. Having killed Old John Coppinger and Amundson, and pushed Frank towards the hang rope, all that had remained was to destroy the ranch he himself had cherished but could not have.

Frank picked up the tracks of the fugitive's horse easily enough. Dodson was clearly not anticipating pursuit at this stage. Once, when Frank was following along a high ridge, he glimpsed his enemy some miles ahead, crossing over a valley, and his pulse quickened. It was bad to have hate inside him like he did, but he could not help it. Dodson had been responsible for so much of the disaster that had smitten him.

The roan was weary and still spooked by the fire. It had been driven too hard for too long, but the last thing he wanted was for Dodson to surge so far ahead that he'd lose him. They'd now entered the wildest terrain imaginable, rocky badlands that rose and fell like immense furrows in a ploughed meadow. Dodson was heading directly across these. Dusk was now slipping in, which, in addition to hiding any sign left, could also pose the threat that Frank might blunder into his prey, not realizing that he had stopped.

Alternatively, if Dodson crossed the badlands successfully, he might make it to Denver in Colorado. There, he would get the opportunity to board a train for the north and disappear forever.

Frank would never cease to think of the man as 'Dodson', but the truth was he was Cyrus Coppinger, the true nephew of Old John Coppinger and perhaps the only person who knew that Frank was an impostor.

This night, there was no moon or stars; thick cloud shrouded the sky. He realized it was pointless blundering on, so he made a halt, camping cold without fire. He had not eaten since leaving Fred Starret's place and now his stomach rumbled — but at least he had a canteen of water which he had topped up at the streams he'd crossed.

He could understand why his horse was so weary, for he felt the same himself. He unsaddled the animal, hobbled its forelegs and left it grazing on the wiry grass. Using his gear as a pillow, he lay back on the hard ground, anxious to get some rest, but anxious to be awake by the first glimmer of dawn, so that he could continue the pursuit.

But sleep would not come, and several times his nerves tensed as sounds impinged upon the silence of the night. He would listen, senses on edge, only to conclude that it was some form of wild life, maybe a mountain cat or the pounce of an owl on an unsuspecting morsel of food.

His mind drifted back. He thought of his wife Lucinda and regretted again everything that had gone wrong between them. He had loved her without a doubt, but their relationship had never been easy, for she had always harboured a discontentment, only deepened by their lack of children. Even so, he could not understand why she had turned to Ty Beddows. He took a deep shuddering breath. He'd encountered more than his fair share of wicked, unscrupulous men. He wondered if he himself was now becoming part of that category. He had entered upon a criminal deception, that he'd hoped would give him an opportunity to escape from the punishment for the crime he'd never committed. But now he knew that one deception only led to another, drawing him deeper and deeper into what seemed a hopeless situation. Although his innocence regarding the theft of cattle had been proved, he was now in a far more dangerous situation than he'd ever been.

And there was Francisca, the Mexican woman. She'd obviously been more deeply involved with events than he'd imagined. And the revelation she'd voiced had shaken him. Old John Coppinger had intended to take Elsa as his young bride. Had her father been manipulating this, so that when the old rancher died, Elsa would inherit the Coppinger ranges, thus bringing the cherished land into the Amundson control? And with the premature death of Coppinger, with the plan thwarted, was that the reason Amundson had tried to marry his daughter off to Frank, whom he thought was the true inheritor of the Coppinger ranges? Had it all been for the purpose of getting their hands on the land? No, he told himself, no!

Questions pounded in Frank's head, but few answers came.

He snatched only minimal sleep, and was wide awake at the first glimmer of dawn. He refreshed himself with water, then saddled the roan, mounted up and pressed on, scanning the ground for sign. At first, he found none and desperation rose in him. Perhaps Dodson had already given him the slip. But round about ten o'clock, with the cold wind snatching at him, he discovered the remnants of a small fire in a dry gully, and surmised that this was where Dodson had stopped during the night. He dismounted, tested the ashes. They were still warm. The fire would have been glowing maybe a couple of hours ago.

Cautiously, he remounted and edged forwards, his eyes combing the surrounding ridges, his hand ready to grasp the pistol from his belt in an instant.

But all the caution in the world would not have prevented the disaster.

The heavy-calibre shot boomed like a thunderclap, and simultaneously the roan staggered and then buckled beneath him. Instinctively, he dragged his feet from the stirrups as he hammered into the icy ground, but his left leg remained beneath the crushing weight of the animal.

He'd been bushwhacked, pure and simple, and he'd blundered into the trap as hopelessly as a blind man.

But Frank's brain was not reasoning at this stage, he was desperately striving to uncobble his jangling senses, hastened by the fear that another shot might boom off at any second — and this time it would be him, rather than the roan, that the bullet found. The beast must have died instantly.

He felt crushed by the weight of the horse, badly hurt, but he realized that his hand was free to drag the pistol from his belt. With the weapon ready, he remained perfectly still, straining his ears for the first indication that his enemy was approaching. For an age he heard nothing.

Frank was sure he was concealed from his enemy by the bulk of the carcass, but this would provide little protection if Dodson vacated his ridge-cover and came down to investigate the result of his sniping shot. Similarly, his weapon was a heavy calibre rifle against which Frank's pistol would be like a pinprick.

Suddenly the sound came, clearly audible above the heaving of his breath — the purposeful, metallic click of the rifle being re-cocked. It seemed to come from the high ridge to his left — and then the slow, cautious sound of footsteps approaching down the slope. Frank swallowed hard, trying to shrink further behind the covering hulk of the animal. He knew that his trapped leg would prevent him from any sudden bodily movement. Maybe he was a sitting duck — but he was a sitting duck with a gun, and his finger snuggled the trigger.

'I know you're there, Frank Miller!'

The voice was chillingly close, just beyond the mound of dead horse. The words came husky with emotion, recognizable only as Dodson's by their cruel, deadly intent — but there was a weariness about them, — and Frank sensed that he must make the supreme effort. And there was something else. Why had his assailant called him 'Frank Miller'?

Frank sucked in a deep breath, then jerked his torso upwards, disregarding intense pain. He saw the man looming above him like a black vulture and fired. The man's bleak face seemed to disintegrate in a flurry of blood and he was thrown backwards, the big rifle spinning from his grasp. Frank spun the cylinder, fired again, causing the body to jerk with the impact of a second bullet. He grunted with satisfaction as he realized that he had succeeded against overwhelming odds.

But he had little cause for celebration. He was in a wild and lonely place. And his leg was pinned, crushed, trapped, beneath the dead weight of his horse.

Despite his bizarre predicament, another thought probed into his mind. The brief glimpse he'd had of his assailant's face had left an unmistakable impression on him. The man he'd killed had not been Jim Dodson.

★　★　★

He lay back, the tension of knowing he had nearly died within the last few moments, the fact that he'd killed a man throbbing through him. His entire body seemed a mass of pain, of bruising, but the agony in his pinioned leg was the worst, and right now he seemed to lack the strength to start the struggle to extract himself. And now the wind was rising, the snow thickening. Suddenly he became aware of the flap of wings and knew that buzzards were circling, drawn by the taint of fresh blood on the cold air. Soon the scavengers had come to earth, and he could hear them squabbling as they attacked the corpse of the man he'd killed.

How long would it be before they transferred their interest to the horse carcass — and then him?

He tried to reason how any assistance might reach him, but gave up in a swelter of despair. Nobody had known that he had given chase after the arsonist, that he'd followed him into this Godforsaken terrain. Nobody would venture into these badlands unless they had good reason to. He groaned, struggled against the weight of the horse until he fell back, exhausted. My God, he would die a slow and agonizing death here.

The thought sent dizziness through him, but after a while he attempted to quell his panic. He tried to reason out some solution to his problem. Whatever it might be, it would have to be on his own instigation, by his own effort. He wondered if he would still be alive come nightfall.

He felt light-headed, sick. For a moment his mind was haunted by the face of the man he had killed. He'd been so certain all along that he was tracking Dodson, that it had been Dodson who had torched the Coppinger ranch — but he had been wrong. And now as recollection came to him of that final moment when he'd discharged the pistol into the man's face, realization came.

The man he had killed had been . . . Ty Beddows. Ty Beddows who had caused him to be falsely convicted of cattle theft and sent to jail, who had corrupted his wife, absconded with her, abused her, and then callously attacked her.

There would be few tears shed for the passing of Ty Beddows. He probably had a reward on his head, though that did not interest Frank. He had other problems to contend with.

He was conscious that the buzzards had transferred their attention from Beddows' corpse, were now ripping at the horse, squabbling as they plunged their greedy beaks into the flesh, pulling out the bloody entrails, causing the bulk of the beast to move, thus inflicting more pain on Frank's trapped leg.

He feared that the scavengers might not differentiate between a carcass and a human who still somehow clung to life. Indeed, he was afforded the horrifying sight of the birds' heads peering at him over the top of the carcass, wrinkled and naked, their beaks dripping with blood, but he waved his arms, shouted, drove them back.

The tangy smell of horse entrails thickened the air, the squabbling screeches of the birds an awesome cacophony. He moved his hand upon the ground and touched the hard metal of the pistol. He still had several shots left in the chamber. Should the worst come to the worst, a bullet in his head might save him the torture of being disembowelled alive.

It seemed he could feel every stab of beak into the horse's bulk, every jerk, as the birds burrowed deeper and deeper into the beast's innards. And with this came a startling realization: the weight pressing down on his leg was lessening. As flesh and organs were transferred into the gizzards of the scavengers, the burden he bore was diminishing.

He struggled again to free himself, new hope surging through him. At first he met with little success and lay back exhausted. A second attempt brought nothing better — but at the third try, he slipped his foot out of his boot and it came free and he could scarcely believe his fortune. He rolled over, his body full of pain, but elation was flowing through his veins, elation at his newly found freedom, elation that momentarily blinded him to the fact that his troubles were far from over.

★   ★   ★

He spent a good hour recovering. He flexed his leg, wincing at the pain. He massaged it, probing with his fingers, not sure whether it was broken or not. He'd suffered terrible bruising and laceration just below the knee, and as he gingerly stood up and placed his weight upon the leg, pain shot upward into his thigh and he collapsed.

Presently, he extracted his boot from beneath the horse and gingerly eased it on.

He at last managed to stand up and painfully hobbled over to where Ty

Beddows lay. The whole body was a ghastly mess of ripped flesh and the man's innards were almost completely hollowed out. The face had already been blasted to bits by the pistol shot — but even so, Frank had no doubt whatsoever about the man's identity.

Ever since disappearing after the attempted murder of Lucinda, Ty Beddows must have harboured a lust for vengeance which had caused him to trail after Frank, eventually discovering that he was running the Coppinger ranch. He had torched the place, no doubt hoping that Frank was inside.

Limping, gritting his teeth against his agony, he took twenty minutes to find Beddows' horse, tethered in the brush some fifty yards back from the ridge. He calmed the beast, hauled himself awkwardly into the saddle. And shortly he was heading back the way he had come.

16

His leg pained him, not easing in intensity. He wondered where he should head for. It seemed there was little to be gained by returning to the charred ruin of the Coppinger Ranch, and certainly the prospect of going into town was fraught with danger. There, he would still be viewed as a wanted man, a murderer, and summary justice was not something he hankered for. It might well be that the county sheriff had arrived by this time, but as Roberto had been unable to spread word of Frank's innocence with regard to the Amundson murder, he would be wanted both by the law and the unlawful.

So he decided to seek sanctuary at the home of his friend Fred Starret. Of course he was assuming that Fred had made it to the County Seat and alerted the sheriff to events in Calico Crossing. If he had not, then the situation would be more desperate than ever.

It was with much trepidation that he finally approached Starret's place, and, as he drew close, he was relieved to see a light showing. Minutes later he had hailed his friend, slipped wearily from his saddle and gratefully accepted the hospitality offered to him.

Starret explained how he had reached Milton City and informed the sheriff of events. He had then returned home. Apparently the sheriff had been delayed while he obtained a Gatling Gun and enlisted the help of a company of the Kansas National Guard. Once satisfied that his force was strong enough, he had ridden for Calico Crossing where he'd arrested those suspected of killing Marshal Rainbird and his deputy, and restored order.

Frank sighed with relief and was soon relating his own experiences.

Starret examined Frank's leg, cursing at what he saw.

'You best rest up here for a few days,' he said. 'Let that leg do its healin'.'

Frank nodded. He was lucky to have a friend like Starret. He needed time, both for healing and to sort out in his mind what his next course of action should be.

That night, bedded down on the couch in the house's main room, he slept and dreamed of Elsa, that he had at last taken her in his arms to taste the sweetness of her kisses. She was whispering that it was never Old John Coppinger that she'd intended to marry, that the only man she really wanted was him. He awoke, feeling the sweat of passion upon him. Daylight, thickened with motes of dust, was slanting through the window. He could hear the clatter of pans, coming from the kitchen, and with it the aroma of frying bacon.

As he attempted to move he realized how his leg had stiffened. Rising, he placed his feet on the ground and straightened up. He could scarcely hobble. He probed his leg with his fingers. The flesh seemed to have taken on a greenish tinge. The hurt was much worse than yesterday, even when he had been trapped beneath the horse. The main bruising had blackened over the knee and lower leg.

The thought of possible amputation hovered in his mind. He had heard of men, seemingly less injured than he was, who had had their limbs excised during the Civil War. Maybe it was more than rest that he needed. By the morning of the third day at Starret's place, he'd made up his mind. He had to get to the doctor in Calico Crossing. Somehow, he'd have to sneak into town and avoid being spotted by the sheriff and his militia. If he was discovered, he might be arrested on sight, charged with Amundson's murder and may be unable to prove who the real killer was.

Reliable as always, Fred Starret could see how he was suffering every time he attempted movement and immediately offered him help.

'I'll take you to town in the springboard. Won't be no easy ride, but you'd never make it forking a horse.'

Frank nodded his thanks.

Early next morning they set out in the wagon, but they were only half way to town when they were shocked to see a party of militia approaching. Before Starret could turn the wagon aside, the militia were upon them and they were immediately recognized and covered by rifles.

'We heard that Coppinger was hiding out at your place, Starret,' the captain in charge of the militia announced. 'I'm placing you both under arrest.'

'I was just takin' him into town to see the doctor,' Fred Starret explained. 'He's got a badly hurt leg.'

'Maybe,' the captain retorted, 'he'll have more than his leg to worry about when the judge gets through with him! I'm charging him with the murder of Amundson.'

Frank knew it was useless to attempt any explanation right now.

An uncomfortable hour later found Frank and Fred Starret locked in the jailhouse. The county sheriff, a dark bearded man, and several of his deputies as well as a captain of militia, manned the jailhouse — and from what Frank saw as he was brought in, the town seemed to be under martial law.

But now Frank was in no mood to sit back and do nothing. He demanded to be heard, and when the county sheriff appeared, he told him that he was not guilty of murdering Amundson and could prove it.

'How come?' the lawman demanded.

Frank said, 'Roberto and Francisca Silvano work out at Amundson's ranch. They know who committed the murder, and they'll give you the truth. The killer was a man known as Jim Dodson.'

The county sheriff gave a resigned sort of nod, as if he'd heard enough false stories, but he reluctantly agreed to send a man out to bring in the two Mexicans.

'There's something else I better tell you,' Frank went on, and he related how he'd found his ranch in flames, how he'd tracked the arsonist, Ty Beddows, and killed him in self defence. And how he'd injured his leg.

'I knew your ranch had been torched,' the county sheriff nodded, stroking his great black beard. 'An Osage woman came into town. It was lucky I could understand her lingo. She told me she'd worked at your place and saw this stranger turn up. He seemed to go crazy, smashing the house up and settin' fire to everythin'.'

Frank nodded. 'Now I'd be mighty grateful if the doc could do somethin' for my leg. The pain is awful.'

The county sheriff said, 'I guess you're entitled to medical treatment. You need to be fit to stand trial.'

Within twenty minutes, Doctor Newcombe was examining Frank's leg, screwing his face up at what he saw. 'You've taken a terrible crushing,' he said. 'The leg'll wither unless 'something's done pretty quick.'

'You ain't thinkin' about cuttin' it off, are you, Doc?'

'Sometimes it's not an easy choice.' Doctor Newcombe had a grave look on his face. 'Maybe it's a matter of living the remainder of your life in constant misery, or losing the limb and having a good wooden leg fitted. A lot of progress has been made since the Civil War. They can make false limbs almost as good as the originals.'

'Well,' Frank frowned, 'I would have to think very carefully before I decided one way or the other.' He felt his worst fears were being confirmed.

One of the deputies had been listening in on the conversation. As the doctor bandaged the leg and gave Frank some opiates to ease the pain, the man said, 'I guess you better wait the result of the trial before you decide on anythin' desperate.'

In other words, Frank thought, *he's tellin' me not to have my leg cut off if I'm due a hanging.*

The doctor chose to ignore the remark. 'I've got a very good surgeon friend over at Milton City, an ex-army man,' he explained, closing his medical bag. 'I'll ask him to come over for a second opinion. Can't do any harm.'

Frank nodded his thanks. Somehow the prospect of losing his leg seemed worse than losing his life.

★ ★ ★

'I'm sorry I got you into this, Fred,' Frank said. He felt really bad at having landed his good friend in jail, the charge being helping a murderer to evade the law.

Starret shrugged his shoulders. 'You'd have done the same for me. Anyway, when your Mexican friends speak up, we'll both be out of here.'

He spoke truthfully. That evening both Roberto and Francisca were brought into town and spent a good hour being questioned by the county sheriff which culminated with them putting their signatures to sworn statements.

Both prisoners were relieved when their cells were unlocked, their few possessions were returned to them and they were free to go.

Starret helped Frank over to the doctor's. The doctor insisted that Frank remain with him until his surgeon friend arrived. He had already sent a message to the ex-army man and was awaiting a reply. Meanwhile, he considered it best for Frank to receive appropriate medical care which he could provide.

Frank agreed, partly because he felt that he had already caused Fred Starret enough inconvenience, so he shook hands with his friend and watched him depart homeward in the wagon. Doctor Newcombe helped Frank into his surgery and suggested a rate of payment for accommodation and nursing which Frank agreed to pay. He was bedded down straight away and the doctor's wife, Hilda, provided nursing care, serving a hearty supper of beef and beans, but the patient had little appetite.

Dosed with more opiates, Frank spent a peaceful night, though pain in his leg awakened him early. To take his mind away from his suffering, he tried to reason out what the future held for him. More and more he became convinced that he could not continue living the lie of an assumed identity. He had been a fool to step into another man's shoes, although at the time he hadn't realized just how much trouble he was letting himself in for. He felt certain that, once he had confessed to the deception, he would be sentenced to a further term in prison. The thought tormented him, but still the compulsion to come clean over everything would not leave him. But not yet, he told himself, not yet.

At eleven o'clock, ex-army surgeon Amos Gallagher arrived on the morning stage, assuaged his thirst at the saloon, and then went to the home of his friend Doctor Newcombe. Gallagher was a tall beanpole of a man, with bushy eyebrows and a seemingly lipless mouth. He was well into his sixties. Within five minutes of arrival, he had fitted his *pinz-nez* spectacles and was examining Frank's leg, probing the now swollen flesh with his long fingers and making low sounds that did not bode well.

'This is pretty bad, you know,' he said.

He asked for the lamp to be brought closer and with the side of his hand made a line just below the knee. He looked at Doctor Newcombe who nodded his head in confirmation. Forlornness settled over Frank like a heavy blanket.

'Tom,' Gallagher said to Doctor Newcombe, 'we'd better have a word in private.'

Newcombe said, 'Sure, Amos,' and the two men left the room, closing the door behind them.

Frank lay back on his bed, conscious of the pain throbbing through his leg. He felt nauseous and trapped. All too soon, it seemed, the door knob was turning and Amos Gallagher re-entered. He reached out and took hold of Frank's hand, as if such a deed would make his words more palatable.

'The choice is yours,' he said. 'My advice would be to have the lower part of your leg amputated. On recovery, the pain would be minimal. I would be happy to do the job. The alternative would be considerable pain, at times agony, if you retain the leg. Already, there maybe gangrene and you could die prematurely. I would advise you to come to my infirmary in Milton City where I would do the job.'

Frank's head slumped. He could hear his heart beating — *thump, thump*. Gallagher was waiting for his reply. After a moment, the impatience of a cough sounded in his throat.

'Do I really have any choice?' Frank at last asked.

222

'Not if you want to live to a normal age, I'm afraid.'

Frank swallowed hard, then in a voice scarcely audible, he said, 'Very well, Doctor. I guess I'm in your hands.'

17

To divert his mind from his physical pain and predicament, Frank forced his thoughts on to other matters. After the surgeon had left, Doctor Newcombe dosed Frank up with opiates, so that he drifted in and out of sensibility, not too certain whether he was dreaming or really experiencing events circulating about his bedside. Somehow, Elsa Amundson probed into his thoughts and he wondered how she was faring, how she had taken the death of her father, and whether it was she who was now ruling the roost at the ranch. Or maybe she had stayed with her aunt. He realized how little he knew about her, and yet her mere physical presence had stirred some emotion in him he could not explain. He also wondered about Jim Dodson and whether he had fled the territory. Or was he still prowling around, intent on making further mischief? Having murdered her father, would he now turn his evil upon Elsa? There were so many questions to which his befuddled brain could find no answers.

While he awaited the call from Amos Gallagher for surgery, he was visited by Roberto and Francisca Silvano, who were greatly concerned about his injury.

'Elsa has come home,' Roberto confirmed.

'How's she taken the death of her father?' Frank enquired.

Roberto shrugged his shoulders. 'She's a very practical woman. She enjoys being the boss, runs a very tight outfit. The truth is, she always called the tune, even when her father was alive.'

Francisca leaned forward, her dark face troubled. '*Señor*,' she murmured, 'there is something I must tell you, something that will not rest in me. I was very fond of John Coppinger. He was very kind to Roberto and me, when we needed help. He was like a father to me. Many people did not like him, but we knew that he was a good man.'

Frank nodded, wondering what she was getting at.

'When he was murdered,' she went on, 'Roberto and me . . . well, our hearts were broken. After he had been shot, I held him in my arms, but I knew he was dying. He told me the name of the one who had shot him. It was Cyrus Coppinger, his nephew. And Roberto and I swore we would avenge his death. Meanwhile, we went to work for *Señor* Amundson.'

'I see,' Frank said, and the inkling of her next words was stirring in his mind.

'When we heard that Cyrus Coppinger had come to town, was in the saloon, we knew what we had to do. What we did not realize was that you were a different Cyrus Coppinger. So Roberto and me . . . we waited for you to walk into the street and . . . '

'You took a shot at me,' Frank said.

'*Sí, Señor.* We are sorry for what we did. We ask for your forgiveness.'

Frank took a deep breath. So that was one mystery less. 'You gave me a mighty bad scare at the time,' he said. 'Ruined my new hat as well.'

'But do you forgive us?' she persisted.

He smiled. 'Guess I'd better. Otherwise you might try it again. And there's something I best tell you. My name isn't Cyrus Coppinger, never was.'

And in brief terms, he explained the truth, the circumstances which had led him to assume the identity of the man who was, in reality, the man known as Jim Dodson.

They were both astonished at what they heard, but they swore that they would not reveal the story to anybody else.

Frank said, 'I think I'll have to tell the sheriff the truth. I can't live with a lie for the rest of my life. Maybe the law will go easy on a man who's just had his leg amputated.'

'You should see another medicine

man,' Francisca said. 'There may be other ways.'

Frank shook his head despairingly. 'I sure wish there were.'

When the Mexicans left, Doctor Newcombe administered more opiates, and Frank slipped into a blissful sleep.

The following morning, Francisca returned. With her was the Osage woman, Maria. She had escaped when the ranch had been set ablaze, and now greeted Frank with considerable affection. She gabbled away in her Sioux language, which was totally incomprehensible to Frank, but Francisca had some knowledge of the tongue and she translated the Indian woman's words.

Her uncle, called Great Bird, was a shaman, a medicine man, of some repute. Maria said that Frank should not have his leg amputated, but should allow Great Bird to treat him.

Frank was ready to try anything. He was fond of his leg, immensely fond and he accepted the suggestion willingly. That afternoon, Francisca and

Roberto arrived at the surgery in a springboard wagon. Frank thanked Doctor Newcombe for all he had done and asked him to inform Amos Gallagher that he was trying an alternative treatment. Newcombe advised Frank against his decision, saying it could cost him his life, but Frank remained determined.

The plan was that he would go to Fred Starret's place, and Great Bird would visit him there. The mere thought that he might not be destined for the surgeon's knife had already given Frank a mental boost, a new optimism. His Mexican friends helped him to the wagon and they left town, Roberto taking great care to ensure a smooth ride.

★   ★   ★

It was three days later that the wizened Osage shaman Great Bird visited Frank. The old Indian wore a hat of fraying straw, with an eagle feather stuck in its band. He looked about a hundred years old and spoke no English. He examined his leg. He did not seem shocked by what he saw, but nodded sagely. The following day, he applied a poultice of skunk cabbage and wild tobacco leaves, so hot it made Frank wince, and dosed him a mixture of herbal remedies, together with countless cups of peyote bean and willow-bark tea to ease the pain. He fumigated the room with sage, allowing the smoke to drift over the patient while he repeated various incantations. He returned twice a day to renew the poultice and repeat the incantations. And Frank lay back and wondered how on earth these weird practices could bring him benefit. But day by day his pain lessened and suddenly hope gave him additional strength.

Sometimes he thought of Elsa and wondered why she did not visit him or even send him a message. Was she still so incensed with him?

*   *   *

Two weeks into Frank's treatment, the mailman delivered a letter. For a moment he hoped it might be from Elsa, but it was not. It was from his wife, Lucinda. It was addressed to Cyrus Coppinger. Frank had told her to address mail thus. He sighed and opened it. He felt bad about Lucinda, but it was Elsa who haunted his dreams.

My Dearest Frank
You know I am not good with words and writing letters, but I can tell you what I say over and over to myself. Thank God, I am recovering from my injury. Doctor says I will be back fully fit soon. But I don't feel so good. I need to be with you again. I am really sorry for what I did. I did not realize how lucky I was to have you for my husband. I love you and always will, and beg you to let us try

*again. I am older and wiser now
— and I say again, I love you.
Yours in hope
Lucinda.*

He read the letter twice, his heart growing heavier by the second, then he carefully folded it before letting it slip through his fingers into the fire.

18

It was three months later and the first stirrings of spring were sweetening the land. Elsa was pumping water from the well in her ranch yard when she was surprised by a voice from behind her. She turned to see a man whose face was hideously scarred down the left side.

'Now Elsa Amundson,' he said, 'we're two of a kind. Both as ugly as sin!'

She dropped the pail she was holding with a clatter. 'Dodson!' she exclaimed. 'I thought you had vanished into thin air.'

'Nearly did. Got burned when some maniac torched the Coppinger Ranch. Lucky to drag myself out alive.'

'What were you doing there?'

'Collectin' bits and pieces. Things that were rightly mine.'

'Well, there's nothing here for you.'

'Oh yes there is.'

'What?'

'You,' he said. 'Like I said, we're two of a kind. At least you can take care of me and provide a man's needs. That's if you want to live.'

She felt terror run through her. This man was mad. His eyes licked over her body like flame, his breathing rapid.

'I'm not coming with you,' she said. 'This is my home, my ranch, left to me by my father.'

'I'm not askin' you to come with me, Elsa. I'm gonna stay here with you. You maybe have worked things out by now. I mean the fact that I'm the real Cyrus Coppinger. That other fella's a damned fake. He squirmed his way in to get his hands on my uncle's money and the ranch. But his game's up now. His ranch house is burned down and he's gonna get what he deserves.'

'So why do you come here?'

'Because,' he said, 'I need somewhere to lie low, get over these damned burns as best I can. And there's somethin' else.'

'What?' she asked suspiciously.

'I want you to be my wife!'

'I'd rather be dead,' she gasped.

'Oh no you wouldn't. I know one thing matters to you, just as it did to your old man. The Coppinger range with all its water. If you got that land, your cattle spread would be the biggest in Kansas. That's what you always wanted.'

'That may be true, but . . . '

'Well,' he interrupted, 'I'm the rightful owner of that land, always have been. You and me, in partnership, could really make somethin' of the combined ranges. And I'll make a promise. I'll make out a will, make sure everythin' is left to you. Then, if anythin' happened to me, it would all be yours. Nobody could take it away from you.'

'You're crazy,' she cried.

He jumped forward, his obvious insanity confirming her worst fears. He grabbed her arm, ripping her blouse. 'I may be a wreck of a man now, but I'm still stronger than any woman!'

She struggled against him, screaming, kicking, but at that moment Roberto, holding a rifle, called out from the porch. 'Leave her alone!'

Dodson momentarily released Elsa, snatched his gun from its holster and fired at the Mexican, sending him plunging backwards in a flurry of blood. Coming from the house, Francisca screamed and ran to her fallen husband.

Elsa erupted in fury. She threw herself at Dodson, hammering on his chest with her fists, but with a great swipe of his arm, he lashed her savagely across the face, sent her reeling away to lie unmoving on the ground.

'You have killed Roberto!' Francisca's shriek had Dodson spinning around to see her with her husband's rifle held in trembling hands.

He unleashed an oath. As he sprang towards her, she pulled the trigger, but the weapon had no bullet in the breech, all it emitted was a harmless click.

Dodson laughed callously and lashed at Francisca, throwing her to the ground in the same way he had done Elsa. She lay unmoving, a thin trickle of blood running from her head across the earth.

Dodson turned back to Elsa. She was beginning to stir, groaning as she did so. He scooped, seized hold of her and dragged her to her feet, supporting her as she swayed. Then he swung her into his arms bodily and carried her up the steps and into the house where he dumped her on a sofa.

Her eyes were open. She gazed at him blankly, showing no emotion. 'If you stay here, the law will come and arrest you for the murder of my father.'

'No,' he laughed. 'Nobody will know I'm here, not for the time bein' anyway.'

'The range hands,' she argued. 'They'll recognize you.'

'I know they've been paid off. Anybody left, fire them. We can soon get a new crew.'

For a moment she just gazed at him, but her brain was working fast. At last her purple eyes narrowed with crafty speculation.

'And after we're married,' she said, 'you'll make out a will, make sure I inherit all the Coppinger land?'

'Sure I will. It'll all be yours one day, that's if you live longer than I do.'

She fingered the ugly bruising on her face, then she nodded.

Dodson grinned, started to speak but then stopped. They both heard the brief murmur of a voice from outside. Dodson moved to the doorway, gazed out. He saw the lifeless body of Roberto sprawled where it had fallen. His wife was leaning over him, weeping. He drew his gun, pointed it at her.

'Get into the house, you Mexican bitch,' he snarled.

She gazed up at him, emitted a sob. The side of her face glistened with blood. Then slowly she straightened up. 'You will pay for this,' she hissed. Shufflingly, she climbed the steps on to the porch and he followed.

'If either of you betray me in any way,' he said, 'I will kill the other one. Remember that.'

The two women gazed at him but said nothing.

He believed that the voice he had heard, had been that of Francisca speaking to the spirit of her dead husband. He was wrong. He had heard Francisca all right — but she had been issuing a sharp order to Ed McMullen, a stable hand, who had heard the shot and come running.

'Get the law — quick — now!' Francisca had instructed.

'But . . .'

'Go now!' and her wide, terror-filled eyes had been enough to send the boy darting away.

★   ★   ★

As he rode to fetch the sheriff from Calico Crossing, Ed McMullen's horse stepped into a gopher hole and the boy

239

was thrown from his saddle. He was badly shaken up, and it took him some twenty minutes before he was able to recapture his animal and remount. His shoulder hurt every time he was jolted. He rode close to Fred Starret's place and saw Fred in a corral, breaking in a horse.

He reined in, breathlessly explained events to Fred. Frank, hearing voices, stepped out of the house onto the porch, glad that he could at least put weight on his injured leg. In fact the last two mornings, he'd chopped wood for Fred and taken a ride. He would be eternally grateful to Great Bird. He heard the boy's words and immediately returned to the house, picked up his gunbelt and strapped it on. Elsa was in extreme danger. He couldn't stand by and do nothing any longer.

Meanwhile Fred had told the boy how bad he looked, and how he better rest up until he felt better. 'I'll ride and get the sheriff,' he said.

By the time Starret had prepared for

his journey, Frank had saddled a horse and had mounted up.

'Where you goin'?' Fred demanded.

'I'm riding for the Amundson place,' Frank explained. 'I guess I got a score to settle.'

'But . . .'

'I'll be all right, Fred,' Frank said. 'You just get the law alerted as soon as you can.'

'Here,' Fred said, unbuckling his gunbelt, 'you take this. You'll need the extra artillery more than me.'

* * *

Frank reached the Amundson ranch house in mid-afternoon. The place had a forlorn and gaunt silence about it. He realized that all the window shutters were fastened across and the door was firmly closed with an inhospitable air about it. A patch of dark earth caught his eye in the yard, and he immediately knew it was blood — Roberto's blood. He swallowed back his grief. The

Mexican had been a good friend.

But where were Francisca . . . and Elsa? Had they suffered a similar fate? And where was Dodson — the instigator of all this tragedy?

Frank had reined in some hundred yards from the house, viewing it between the surrounding barns. His enemy could be hiding anywhere, watching out with his gun ready. Unless he'd disappeared, taking the women with him as hostages. Frank had to find out. If he waited too long, it would be nightfall and under cover of darkness the situation could be even more dangerous.

He dismounted, wincing as his leg took the weight. It would probably cause him pain for years, if he survived the next few hours, but he was thankful that he had escaped Amos Gallagher's surgical knife. He'd always had a sneaking suspicion that surgeons enjoyed their work too much. But now he turned his mind to other things.

Leaving the horse and drawing one of

his guns, he checked that the chamber was loaded and crept forward, keeping close to the outside of the barn walls. Soon he would have to cross the open yard and that was when he would be most at risk.

He froze as he heard a sound from the roof of the ranch house and he glanced up. He crouched down, conscious of the pound of his heart. Maybe Dodson was up there. But straining his eyes as much as he could, he found himself squinting into the sun. Suddenly he saw a big black crow flapping skyward from the roof and he wondered what, if anything, had scared the bird. The roof was surrounded by a low balustrade, suitable for a man to crouch behind if he was so inclined.

Frank weighed up his chances, having an urge to reach the house and discover what carnage was inside — perhaps the dead bodies of the women. The thought sickened him. The open yard lay before him, seemingly innocuous yet an obvious killing ground for a waiting gunman. Beyond it were the steps that led up to the porch and the main door.

A sudden impatience boiled inside Frank and he decided to chance his luck. Rising to his feet, he sucked in a deep breath, then made his run, trying to ignore the pain in his leg. He was only half way across the yard when the gun cracked out from the roof of the house. Simultaneously, a bullet sliced through his left shoulder muscle, sent him spinning around and down. Immediately a second shot came, and he felt a brutal slam against his ribs and with it a scorching sensation that cut his breath. He sensed that a third shot would finish him. He clawed his way onto his feet, forced himself forward and reached the covering of the porch.

In his frantic rush to escape the line of fire, he had dropped his gun. It lay in the middle of the yard, clear for anybody to see. His enemy might now think that he was unarmed, an easy prey to pick off. He was thankful that

Fred Starret had given him a second pistol. He rapidly drew it from its leather and confirmed it was charged.

He guessed that Dodson was somewhere above him on the roof, but he surely had an internal means of access and could therefore descend whenever he chose. Frank strained his ears for the slightest give-away sound, but he heard nothing. Now for the first time, he could feel pain throbbing down his left arm, and he realized that his shirt sleeve was sodden with blood. Dodson's first bullet had caught his shoulder. As for the second shot, it had exploded a cartridge in his gunbelt, scorching his ribs as it burst. The immediate numbness had given way to pain and stiffness. If it came to a physical fight, he feared he would be at a distinct disadvantage.

Suddenly he heard a thumping sound from within the house — the upper floor. It was as if somebody was pounding on a door. And then a woman shrieked and he knew it was Elsa. He groaned. What was Dodson doing to her?

Gun poised, he rose from his crouching position, moved across the porch, cursing as the boards creaked beneath his feet. He realized that he was leaving a trail of blood behind him, plain for all to see. He reached the door, grasped the brass handle and turned it. The door opened inwardly, revealing the darkened main room, the shuttered windows turning it into a deep sea of shadow. Conscious that he was silhouetted in the doorway, he slipped inside, and quietly closed the door behind him, plunging the room into darkness. He pressed his back against the wall, then crouched down, anxious to make himself as small a target as possible; he had the sour, bitter taste of fear in his mouth.

The thumping sound from upstairs had ceased; Elsa had been silenced. But now he heard a board creak from the landing, followed by the sound, quiet and secretive, of somebody creeping down the staircase. His finger was curled inside his trigger guard, the gun held away from his body, his eyes adjusting to the various degrees of darkness. His hands felt slippery with sweat, or was it blood? In fact his entire body was oozing sweat, turning him ice-cold.

Moments passed in blackness. He remained motionless, crouched like a dog-wolf, the breath locked in his throat, but his heart was pounding overtime.

Suddenly the silence was ripped open by the thunderous roar of a gun and lead tore into the wall inches above his head. He'd been saved by his crouch. His ears deafened by blast, his eyes half blinded by the sudden illumination of the fired gun, he none the less glimpsed a shadowy movement; somebody was crouching on the stairs, scarcely fifteen feet away. He fingered his own trigger, fired. The reverberation of the shots filled the room, the air thickened with acrid smoke. As darkness returned, he knew that he had done no more damage than splinter the banister wood.

He moved quickly, knowing that any doubts Dodson had had about him being unarmed were quashed. Now each man knew the other was in lethal proximity, armed and ready to kill. Ducking low, Frank changed his position, but despite his efforts to subdue sound, he blundered into a chair, sending it crashing over, and almost immediately the room was again illuminated by a thundering flash. He winced as he felt the skim of lead close to his sweat-slicked neck. He retaliated, firing off two quick shots and rolled to the side, finding himself between the legs of a table. Entwined with the deafening echo of the gunblast and the crash of falling crockery from a dresser, he heard a man's pitiful groaning, eventually cut off by a choking sound.

He would have fired again, but the hammer fell on a spent casing.

He waited for what seemed an

eternity, poised perfectly still as the ring of the gunfire in the closed room subsided. He suspected that Dodson was playing dead, planning to trick him. He waited some more, then he was startled by the renewed thumping coming from the upper floor.

Gingerly, he roused himself, paused, tense and ready. With trembling hands, he recocked his gun, then stepped across to the outer door. He opened it, and in the light that flooded in, he saw the motionless Dodson sitting on the floor, back against the dresser, a mass of smashed crockery about him on the floor. Frank moved across, aiming his gun at Dodson's head, suspicious that the man might leap up with his weapon blazing. But he did not. His throat was all bloody, ripped open by lead. His handgun lay on the floor amid the crockery. Frank prodded the body with his boot. It toppled over, bending at the waist, as if it were top heavy. Frank stooped, checked, and knew that Jim Dodson was dead, but even in death an evil leer showed on his scorched features. Frank was shocked by the man's changed appearance and the way his flesh had been burned, but he felt no sympathy.

The upstairs thumping was growing more intense.

He mounted the stairs, hobbling on his weakened leg, moved along the landing, opening a set of shutters as he went, and came to the heavy oak door that was trembling under the rain of blows that pounded it from the other side.

The key was still on the outside of the door. He turned it, and a moment later the door was opened to reveal the flush-faced Elsa Amundson and behind her a dazed looking Francisca Silvano.

'Where is he?' Elsa demanded. 'He locked us in.'

Frank looked for relief, for gratitude in her scarred face, but saw only anger.

'He's dead,' he said. 'He tried to kill me, but I got him first.'

'You are wounded, *Señor*.' It was

Francisca showing concern.

Frank had forgotten. He looked down at his blood soaked sleeve. 'It'll heal, nothing serious,' he said. 'Francisca, I'm real sorry about Roberto. He was a good man.'

She nodded, tears glinting in her eyes, but she said, 'Let me bandage that shoulder. It will slow the bleeding.'

He swung towards Elsa. 'You all right?'

All of them now heard the sound of hoofs from outside. Frank moved across to the window and looked out.

'It's the sheriff's posse,' he said. 'Better late than never, I guess.' Then again he faced Elsa and repeated his question. 'You all right?'

He would never forget the hatred that blazed from her eyes, the absolute venom. Her scar seemed to have turned a furious red. All at once she seemed to him like a merciless reptile.

'*Imposter!*' she spat at him.

19

After the gunfight at the Amundson Ranch and the killing of Jim Dodson who, in truth, was the real Cyrus Coppinger, Frank Miller spent four weeks with his good friend Fred Starret, recovering from the bullet wound he'd suffered. He'd been incredibly lucky. The lead had done nothing worse than leave a groove in the flesh of his shoulder. Of course the strain he'd placed upon his leg had done it no favours, but, with rest, his recovery continued.

He had learned how Dodson had nearly been burned to death in the fire at the Coppinger Ranch. He had been a crazy killer, but the brush with his own death and the horrific burns he'd suffered had completely unhinged his brain, leaving him with intent only for revenge on those whom he considered had wronged him.

During his inactivity, Frank pondered on his affairs more and more. He would never forget the black abhorrence that had flared in Elsa Amundson's eyes and the sting of her venomous rebuke — *imposter!* He had totally mistaken her intentions. Now he realized that she had never harboured the slightest affection for him. Her desires had encompassed nothing but a ruthless greed for land, something she had shared with her father.

Now Frank felt a repulsion, both for her and himself. He had no wish to ever see her again, in fact the further she was away from him the better. As for himself, he had blundered into sinful ways, pushed partly by fate, but even more so by his own deviousness. He no longer wanted to live a lie; he wanted to atone for what he had done, to distance himself from his own past. He talked about it at length with Fred Starret who tried to dissuade him from what was in his mind, saying time would heal over the wrong doings and folks would attach little importance to the truth, even if they knew about it. But matters would not rest in Frank's mind, and a month to the day after the killing of Dodson, he wrote out a statement which he addressed 'To whom it may concern, c/o Elliot Freshman, Attorney at Law, Calico Crossing'.

He chose his words carefully:

I hereby relinquish all claim to the land, any remaining property, and sums of money previously belonging to Mister John Coppinger. I request that full search should be carried out for any true descendant or relative of John Coppinger and that the estate should be passed to said person.
Signed:
Frank Miller
(Falsely known as Cyrus Coppinger)

Next morning, he bade farewell to Fred Starret, touched by the tear he saw in the old man's eye. He personally delivered his written statement to Elliot Freshman's office in Calico Crossing, but left before the legal man had read it, having no wish to enter into discussion. He boarded the morning stage, and as it rolled out of town, he shuffled words around in his mind, trying to compose his feelings. *Time to forget the past . . . I am on my way home . . . We must start afresh, realize that we were both at fault, and pray to make a better go of things in future.*

Before he boarded the north-bound train in Milton City, he put the words into coherent form and telegraphed them to his wife Lucinda in Wyoming. He prayed that it would be the wisest nine dollars he'd ever spent.

THE END